AF227853

DINING
WITH DEVILS

BOBBY CREW

"Hell is empty and all the devils are here."
— WILLIAM SHAKESPEARE,
The Tempest

The Horror Crew Productions, LLC
www.TheHorrorCrew.com
info@TheHorrorCrew.com

© 2019 by Robert Crew
All rights reserved

No part of this book may be reproduced in any written, electronic, recording, or photocopying form without written permission from the publisher: the exception would be in the case of brief quotations embodied in critical articles or reviews and pages where permission is specifically granted by the publisher.

Books may be purchased in quantity and/or special sales by contacting the publisher directly.

The Horror Crew Productions LLC, Denver, Colorado
717 17th Street, Suite 1900 #147, Denver, Colorado, 80202
info@thehorrowcrew.com

Editing by: Barb Wilson & Jen Zelinger
Cover Design & Interior by: Kelsey Owens, KAOS Design

ISBN: 978-1-7330829-0-7 (Soft Cover)
ISBN: 978-1-7330829-1-4 (Hard Cover)
ISBN: 978-1-7330829-2-1 (eBook)
LCCN: 2019908369

Fiction | Horror | LGBTQ | Mystery, Thriller and Suspense

First Edition

THE COLLECTION

A DATE WITH A DEVIL

Do people really call you Wolf?" Scarlett was sitting across from me at the white cloth-covered table, sipping a Bordeaux blend from the biggest wine glass I'd ever seen. Apparently, there are large glasses designed specifically for the high-end French wine.

The fancy place wasn't at all my scene, but if wining and dining her was going to make her less of a pain when I tore into her with my teeth, I was willing to compensate. Even people on death row got a last good meal, so why shouldn't pretty girls?

I stared into her honey-colored eyes a bit too long, and she averted her gaze. I made her nervous, and I had no shame in exploiting it. She was shy, but she wanted it bad. I could tell just by looking at her—everything from the way she stared at me when she thought I wasn't paying attention, the way she kept fidgeting in her chair, the crimson sundress she wore that complemented her dark skin, and those perfect black curls around her head. She had done her best to look perfect for me.

"That they do," I finally said with a smirk. I gripped the double IPA tightly in my hand. I drank it straight from the bottle, ignoring the frosty glass the waiter had tried to give me.

"I got the nickname when I was younger. I used to growl and howl a lot when I was a kid."

"Sounds kind of adorable." Her voice was a little high, but filled with sweetness.

Every inch of her radiated both childlike innocence and temptation.

"What can I say? I'm a real animal," I almost growled.

She giggled. "I don't think you are all that bad. I think there's a sweet guy in there, underneath all your fur and tattoos."

You'd like to think that, my little pet, but I'm as bad as they come.

I half-smiled at her attempt to make herself feel safer and normalize me. Most people were intimidated by my presence. I am six foot six, a solid foot taller than her, and I worked hard on my rock-hard body. I kept my hair long, and the ladies loved it. My arms were full sleeves, and tats covered most of the rest of my body as well. My ink consisted mostly of nature's most deadly predators, including a dire wolf howling at the moon. I also had one of those faces where my default expression was anger. Angry, hungry, and horny—those three words pretty much summed up my entire existence.

"I know what you're thinking," she said. "You think I'm just young and naïve, that I have no idea what I'm talking about, and that you are a bad boy. You guys seem to think us girls will fall for it."

You already have, I thought.

"You don't like bad boys? You seem to be pretty into me so far, and things have only just begun."

I knew her type, a typical woman who craved the bad boy and always stupidly fooled herself into thinking that she could tame or train him.

"I'll admit, my track record has been pretty bad so far …" She seemed to be talking more to herself than to me, but her tone was optimistic. She met my gaze.

"Men can be brute creatures, and I suppose I used to rely on greater beasts to take care of me, as I didn't really care for myself. But now I know who I am, I know what I want, and no, I have no intention of trying to tame you, Mr. Wolf."

She said it as if she knew what I was thinking.

"My ex, he was rather obsessed and a bit abusive, but in a way he taught me a lot."

Her voice was suddenly filled with regret.

"He was kind of a …" She shook her head, "We shouldn't be talking about exes on our first date anyway. I'm sorry."

"Agreed," I said.

I sure wasn't about to talk about my exes. I didn't exactly have exes anyway; none lasted long enough to qualify. Poor things, they always died too soon. Instead of exes, I had a body count, bodies with so little left of them that no one would ever be able to identify them.

"In fact, we don't ever have to have the exes talk," I said. "Your past doesn't matter to me. Live in the moment, as you never know when it will be your last."

"Cheers to pasts forgotten," she said, raising her wine glass.

I smiled—genuinely this time—and clinked my glass to hers.

The waiter returned and we ordered. She chose the halibut, and I decided on the filet, as rare as they could possibly cook it. I would have eaten the damn thing raw, but societal norms prevented me from indulging. I did, however, order the beef carpaccio as an appetizer.

"So what made you decide to ask me out?" she asked sweetly, fishing for a compliment on her looks.

"Because of the book you were reading," I said sarcastically.

She laughed, "And what book would that be? Let's see how well you were paying attention."

"You were reading *The Great God Pan*," I said smugly. She grinned and nodded her head, both pleased and surprised.

"I'm impressed."

"I'm quite observant."

"Have you read it?"

"No, but I'm somewhat familiar with it, or should I say, with the fact that it wasn't well received in its time.

It was too perverted and dark for people back then. It was an odd choice of literature for coffee in the park reading, and it made me hope that you yourself were odd, if nothing else."

Honestly, it had nothing to do with her looks or the book she was reading. It had a lot more to do with the way she smelled. Every person on Earth has a slightly different scent, and hers was more flowery than most. Call me a softy if you want, but I've always been one to stop and smell the roses. I loved her scent. I'd probably keep a piece of her as a token, something to sniff for later.

"You're not quite what I was expecting," she said.

"You mean I'm more intelligent than you were expecting?"

"Not quite that. You're just … different."

"Is that a compliment?"

"I'm still deciding," she teased.

"Well, you are exactly what I was expecting."

"Yeah? And who exactly am I?"

"Smart, pretty, and recently emancipated from the trials of relying on a man to take care of you. You're career-focused; we haven't really talked about your career, but I'm just going to make this assumption. You live alone, and do a lot of things alone, you might have a cat, and you probably come here once a week with your girlfriends for happy hour; and when I say girlfriends, I mean your coworkers. You're a local, born and raised here, and you think about moving away, yet you're still attached to the place for whatever reason, and yes, you are a little odd. How am I doing so far?"

"A little too good," she said.

"What's your cat's name?"

"Misha."

I'd probably kill her cat first. Maybe I'd do it in front of her. I'll also admit that I am childish and never learned not to play with my food, and oh, did I love to play.

The last girl—Sady—she had been a real treat. I fucked her, as I normally do before killing them. Sometimes I killed them right away, and sometimes I chained them up for awhile, and made them worship me. I'd nip off little pieces of them until they complied. Sady, however, I decided to let free. I felt like a good chase, so I let her run through the woods for awhile.

I stalked her. It was easy. I didn't even have to sniff her out, she was so loud with all the screaming. It wasn't a good hunt, but it was amusing enough to satiate my inner puppy. I had caught her, thrown her down, and bitten off a finger.

She squealed in agony, and then I let her run again. I continued to catch her, tackle her, bite off another piece of her, and then released her. I did it until she collapsed from both exhaustion and blood loss. Then I finally ate my fill. I loved the smell people give off when their body is under stress and afraid. Their aroma is so strong, and it makes them taste a whole lot better. It's like a marinade: the longer they scream, the greater the flavor.

Before her, I found a skinny, hairless twink named Rodger who was on a hunt for a daddy. I didn't have to do anything to lure him in except stand there. A gay bar is like an all- you-can-eat buffet. They couldn't keep their hands off me, stroking my muscles and yes, my ego.

I didn't discriminate; no racial or gender hang-ups here. Why would I deny myself a bouquet of flavor?

I actually let Rodger live for a few days. I let him play out his servant-and-master fantasy for a while; he was great at it. He lived only to please me, but then it came time to make him scream for me in a different way. I broke his ribs one by one and pulled them from his chest before shoving my whole face into his stomach and devouring his insides.

"Earth to Wolf," Scarlett called.

"Sorry, I was off in my head."

"I saw that. I take it you didn't even hear my question."

"I did. I was just thinking about my answer."

She'd asked me where I saw myself in five years. I'm sure she was hoping that I'd say I'd have settled down by then, gotten married and had a kid. But that wasn't what I had planned. Not anytime soon at least. Not unless I found someone who loved the thrill of the hunt as much as I did. The woman who would fuck me while covered in the innards of our kill, that was the woman I planned to marry. Unfortunately, that was incredibly difficult to find.

"I guess I see myself traveling the world."

"I love it," she said. "Have you been able to travel much?"

"I've been all over the states, South and Central America, and Canada. I speak fluent Spanish. I want to make it overseas, though. That's next on my list."

She smiled dreamily. "I'm the opposite. I've only visited a few states, but I've been to several countries in Europe and Africa. Central and South America are next on my list. I love learning about the oldest of civilizations, so when I travel, it's usually to learn. I'm a history major, and in grad school I specialized in mythology and religious studies. There are so many different belief systems out there; it's really incredible. I like hunting for both the similarities and the oddities."

"Are you religious?"

"I guess you could say that," she said. "But not in a traditional sense. I understand that religion developed in mankind's attempt to understand the world around them, to explain the unexplainable, and thousands of years ago there were a lot of unexplainable things, like tornados and lightning. But most of all, it was our attempt to understand death. What happens when we die? That's the great, terrifying mystery."

"Do you fear death?"

"Of course. We all do, don't we? Except for those who have been lulled into believing they have mansions waiting for them in heaven, or multiple chances at life until their spirits evolve and escape the cycle."

"Now you sound like you don't believe in afterlife. Wouldn't that make you …"

"I didn't say I don't believe in an afterlife of sorts. I just said I was afraid of death, and that I know there isn't some mansion waiting for me when I die. I do think this life is as good as it gets, unfortunately. Anyway, enough about my beliefs. Are you religious?"

"Sure. I worship the moon goddess when I howl at night."

"You're taking this wolf thing a bit far now," she murmured with a laugh. "A goddess, huh?"

"Sure, why not? If I'm going to worship anything, it's going to be beautiful, and a woman."

"I understand," she said. "To the goddess of the moon."

She once again held out her glass of wine, now almost empty. I tapped my empty beer bottle with her glass again. We ordered more drinks with our appetizer. She didn't enjoy the carpaccio, which was fine by me. I was starving, and nothing in this restaurant was going to satisfy my hunger.

The waiter dropped dessert menus in front of us after dinner. I said I wasn't interested in the sweets, hoping she would follow suit. She didn't. She ordered the chocolate cake. I cringed. Chocolate always altered the scent and taste a bit. No matter how sweet the chocolate was to others, it was the bitterest tasting thing in the world to me.

I hid my irritation and ordered the crème brûlée. She was halfway through her dessert when she dropped her fork. It clanked loudly against the plate and toppled over onto the floor.

"What's the matter?"

"Remember how I mentioned my ex earlier? I was

going to tell you he's a bit psychotic. He also happens to be sitting at the bar."

I turned toward the bar, and in less than two seconds, I picked him out of the crowd. It wasn't hard. He was staring at us both, glaring.

"I'm really sorry," she said, embarrassed, and almost a little afraid.

I could smell her scent a little stronger already. Her rosy smell was tainted, but she had only made it a couple of bites into her chocolate cake.

"It's not a problem at all," I said seriously. "He looks like a beta anyway."

"A beta?" Her frown became a grin in an instant. "How funny. And I guess that means that you're an alpha?"

"I'll let you decide that for yourself," I said. "But in any case, I'll take care of him if he tries anything. I can't have him hounding my new girl now, can I?"

I wondered why a girl as beautiful as Scarlett would subject herself to someone as inferior to her as the man who was watching us.

"I didn't know you liked older guys. What was he, your sugar daddy?"

"He's only forty-two," she said defensively.

"And we haven't even hit our thirties."

"He's not rich at all. Maybe that would have made the relationship last longer," she joked.

"Want to go do something fun?" I asked.

"If you're trying to lure me back to your place …"

"I was talking about a dive bar outside of town, near

the woods."

"And I was going to suggest my place."

My ears perked up a bit. I wasn't expecting her to be so eager. She didn't even need the slightest convincing. She was probably trying to make her ex jealous, and I had no problem with that.

"It's right on the edge of the woods, actually," she said. "My backyard leads right into a trail that goes deep into the woods. I used to hike there a lot when I was a little girl."

"I'm game." I ordered three shots of tequila and asked the waiter to bring the check along with the alcohol. This took him by surprise, but he didn't protest.

I handed Scarlett one of the tequila shots, and handed the third shot to the waiter, instructing him to deliver it to the guy in the green button-up who couldn't keep his eyes off us. The waiter's face revealed how uncomfortable he was, but he left in the direction of the bar.

Scarlett laughed and took her shot without cheersing me. I slammed my shot and extended my hand. She took another large bite of the chocolate before she placed her gentle hand in mine. I cringed, but she didn't notice. I didn't even bother looking over at her loser ex as I guided her through the crowded dining room and out of the restaurant. The summer night was perfect, just warm enough to not need a jacket.

"Want to follow me?" she asked.

"Or you could just ride on the back of my bike," I pointed to my motorcycle.

"How did I know?" She rolled her eyes.

"I thought I wasn't what you expected."

"I take it back," she said.

"Are you riding or not?"

"Of course I'm riding."

She followed me to my bike, and I handed her a helmet. I never used one, but I figured I'd always keep one on me for whatever poor unsuspecting person who dared come along. She took it, and frowned.

"On second thought …"

"Are you afraid it will mess up your hair?"

"No!" she snapped.

She turned around and looked at the front door. Her ex wandered outside. He had no shame, and wasn't even trying to hide the fact that he was stalking us.

"Whatever, let's just go. At least he won't suspect that we are going to my place if I'm riding with you and abandoning my car."

"Yet he could still just follow us." I kind of hoped that he would follow us.

The thought of going down on her and sinking my fangs between her legs while he watched from the window, as her pleasure transformed into anguish and terror, gave me a stiffy. I'd cripple her, and save her for later, and then hunt him down and tear the bones from his screaming body. God, how I wanted them both …

"He won't follow us if you drive fast enough," she challenged and forced her head into the helmet.

I hopped on the bike, and she clung to my back, her arms wrapped a little too tightly around my waist. We took off in loud dramatic fashion. I glanced back several times, and unfortunately, I didn't see anyone following us.

Despite the noise, she managed to guide me to her house. The directions were easy, but the drive was quite long. She lived far outside of town. Finally, we reached a narrow dirt road that led to an old wooden house that hugged the woods. The house sat on several acres of land.

"This is quite a place you have," I said after turning off the bike. "You must actually make a decent living."

"I inherited this place from my grandmother," she said. "My mom was an only child, and she died before my grandmother, so it was passed down to me, her eldest granddaughter. I grew up here, though. I love it out here."

"I love it too," I admitted.

As the dirt road reached the house, it became a garden walkway. There were rose bushes, lavender bushes, and several different flowers, many of which I didn't recognize.

She took my hand and guided me up the porch steps to the front door. When she opened it, a Siamese cat greeted us at the door with a meow. Her meow quickly turned to a hiss when she saw me.

"Misha, you be sweet," Scarlet scolded.

The cat's hiss turned to a low growl. Scarlet used her foot to nudge the cat outside, and it bolted down the stairs and disappeared under the porch steps.

"Sorry, she's not used to guests. She's kind of a bitch."

"No worries." I wanted to tear the thing's head off,

but I figured I'd wait until after Scarlett got me off. She flicked on the light and motioned for me to enter.

"This is my lovely home."

The smell hit me first. The house smelled as vibrant as her garden outside, yet as rich and crisp as a bookstore. She had more bookshelves than any house I'd ever seen, and whatever free space she had on the walls that wasn't blocked by literature was graced with paintings and prints of sculptures.

I found myself wandering into the living room and ogling her tastes. I recognized the poster of one of the sculptures as Bernini's *Rape of Persephone*. I only knew this because I took a humanities class once, and it immediately became my favorite art piece. The way Hades' hand grips Persephone's thigh gave me chills, and how Bernini managed to incorporate that in a sculpture was nothing short of amazing. She caught me staring at it, and linked her arm with mine.

"There's plenty more where this came from. Would you like a tour?"

I turned to her and kissed her hard on the mouth. The kiss took her by surprise, but she didn't resist. Her tongue entangled with mine, and her scent intensified.

Despite the chocolate, her scent was still intoxicating, and I immediately wanted more. Eventually she pulled away, breathing heavily.

"Down, boy, the night has only just begun. There's no hurry."

She took several steps back and sat down on one of the most comfortable-looking couches I've ever seen. She patted the seat beside her. I obeyed, like a good boy.

I gave the room another once-over and realized that she didn't have a television. Across from the couch was the fireplace, and above it an oil painting of a middle-aged woman who was obviously related to Scarlett. She had similar long black curly hair, and wore fancy old clothes and pearls from the previous century.

"My grandmother," she said, catching me staring at it. "Kind of odd that the painting is there, but I never wanted to move it. It makes me feel closer to her."

"You have her eyes," I said.

"I lucked out on that one," she agreed. "My brother and sister both got my dad's dark eyes."

"She looks like she could be your mother."

"So did my mother," she joked.

"I can't help but notice your lack of electronics."

"I prefer books," she said, motioning to the library around her.

"You're missing out on so many good shows," I said.

"And everyone else misses out on all the good reads."

"I like it." I did like it, but I was still going to kill her. "Have you read them all?"

"Of course not," she laughed. "But it doesn't stop me from growing my collection." She took my hand and her fingers laced with mine. "I think I'll get us some more wine."

"Have anything stronger?"

"Scotch," she said. "Obviously."

"I think I'm in love." I wasn't. Her scent had lightened, and I wanted to get her riled up again.

She got up and left me alone, disappearing through a doorway in the back of the room. I decided to snoop a little and check out her book collection. I did enjoy reading; I just didn't do it often. I was the average college grad who made it to graduation by selectively choosing which books to read, based on whether or not it would affect my grades, not that grades mattered much to me. Back then, I was more interested in finding out which poor little loners would go virtually unnoticed if they disappeared.

Her books seemed to be organized by genre. She seemed to have the entire history of the world in her collection, and she had books on religions I had never even heard off.

"You could borrow one if you'd like," she said, startling me, which is no easy thing to do.

I pride myself on always being aware. I didn't let her know she snuck up on me; I was a bit too prideful for that. She handed me a snifter with a heavy pour of scotch. I graciously took it and sniffed it. It was smoky. I loved it. She sure knew how to treat herself to the luxuries in life. She sipped red wine and stared at me curiously.

"What?"

"Take off your shirt," she said.

I eyed her again, surprised, but I decided to do as she said. Her free hand came out and touched my body. She was inspecting my tats while gently sliding her fingers over my muscles. She paused at a tattoo on my chest of a grizzly bear, and her fingers caressed their way down my abs to my pants line.

I took another sip of Scotch before I set the glass on the bookcase and grabbed her arm and pulled her to me. I kissed her again, and resisted the urge to tear off her dress. My mouth went to her neck, and I bit her a bit harder than I intended. She gasped, and the glass in her hand fell to the wooden floor, shattering and spilling wine over our feet.

I scolded myself for getting carried away, but I didn't apologize. I didn't need to apologize. Fear crossed her face for only a moment before she jumped on me. I stumbled back, my shoulders hitting the bookshelf, and she was in my arms kissing me hard, sliding her teeth across my face, her fingers gripping my hair.

I decided to tear the dress; she wouldn't need it ever again, anyway. I yanked her up and carried her to the couch. I kicked off my boots as I removed her clothes and tasted her breasts.

We rolled around on the couch, tasting every inch of each other. We used our mouths to get each other off before moving to her bedroom. She was insatiable, and her rosy scent kept me going. She let loose a high-pitched moan as I entered her. I bit her hard, and she hardly flinched. I left bruises, teeth marks, and broke her skin.

She bit me back really hard, and she scratched me so hard she drew blood. It stung, but it didn't faze me. I felt like I was floating above us, feeling everything while observing the both of us from above.

She was more aggressive in bed than any woman I'd ever experienced. She rubbed the little spot of my blood over her breasts, and she screamed as she climaxed.

I was close behind.

We lay there for a while, breathing heavy and sweaty. Part of me almost decided to let her live. I wanted it again, but I couldn't resist tasting her, and I couldn't wait any longer. The smell was too intoxicating, and the carnal beast within me raged more than it had in a long time. It wanted her; it wanted to rip open her chest and bury its face into her torso, devouring every organ, to feel the crunch of her bones between its teeth.

I stood up at the foot of the bed, cracked my knuckles, and stretched, and then I felt my bones shift in my body, felt the fur bursting from my skin. Transforming was as agonizing as it was euphoric. I grew even taller, my muscles expanded, my skull and jaws shifted outward, and my fangs erupted out of my snout. I watched as her honey eyes widened as she lay there, frozen in fear on the bed.

I roared and howled, and I pounced.

Only I didn't reach her. My feet didn't leave the ground before I felt searing hot pain in my back. I felt a snap and suddenly I crumpled, half on the floor, half on the bed. I couldn't move. Something heavy was sticking into my flesh and hanging from my back, but I couldn't turn my head to see it. My howl became a pathetic whine.

"Did you really just fuck a werewolf?" a voice asked behind me.

"Mmm hmm." She slithered about on the bed and moaned, as if having another orgasm. "It was the best sex I've ever had, too. Far better than you."

"You really are a bitch."

Whatever object that had impaled me was plucked from my body, and dropped onto the floor. It was an axe. It alone wouldn't kill me. Even with a severed spine, my body could repair itself if given enough time. But time was not on my side.

"Take him to my tub for my bath," she demanded, sitting up in bed.

She clamped her knees together, and then opened her legs before clamping them again slowly, over and over, teasing the man behind me, whom I could only suspect was her ex.

"Try not to waste any more blood than you have to. Drain him dry. His blood is precious, and the ritual bathing should keep me young for years to come."

I was an idiot. How could I have let myself be so stupid? I understood now, but it was much too late. The painting flashed before my mind. It wasn't her grandmother; the likeness had been too perfect. It was her. Her ex must have aged too much for the immortal youth, yet he still longed for her ravishing love, so he stuck around like a pet.

"As you wish," he said bitterly.

He tugged my body, and despite my weight, I toppled helplessly over onto the ground. I heard a meow and a purr in my ear.

It was that damned cat, its eyes aglow. It was lapping up a small pool of my blood. The man dragged my heavy and near-lifeless body off the bed and across the floor like a good, obedient dog. As my head slid across the floor, my eyes caught sight of the Scarlett witch, now crouched on the edge of her bed, smiling at me so sweetly.

She blew me a kiss, and despite my anger, frustration, regret—and yes, my fear of the final darkness that awaited me in impending death—I felt myself longing for her flowery kiss once more.

A DATE WITH A DEVIL

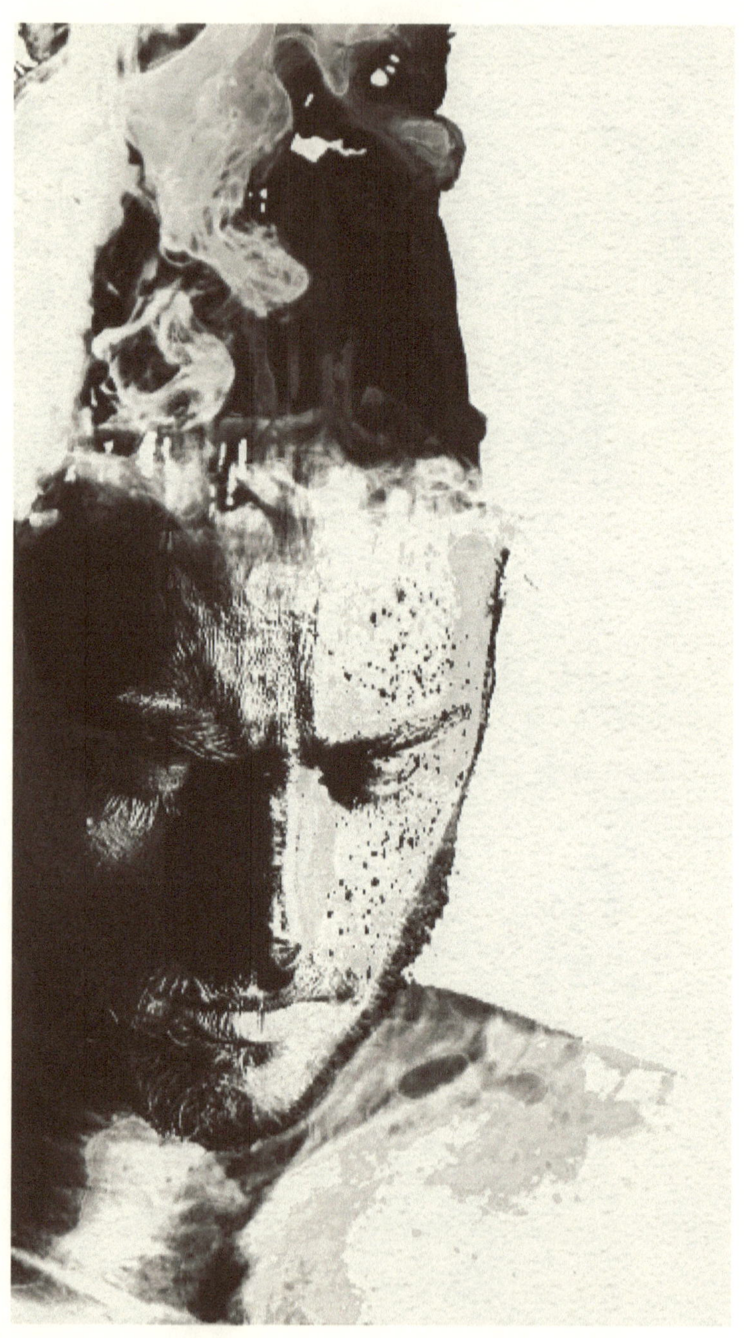

A LETTER TO THE DEAD

In loving memory of a dear friend, one I wrote a letter to after death: a letter that inspired this story. I wish he lived long enough to learn to love himself for who he was.

Nick signed his name at the bottom of the letter and set his pen down on the desk. He resisted the urge to read the words he'd written. He knew if he did, he might cross some of them out. Or worse, he'd tear the paper in half, eliminating the evidence of having poured out all of his emotions in favor of writing some generic words like, "I'll miss you, or you'll be in my heart forever." He sighed, leaned back in his chair, and closed his eyes. Writing the letter had been both liberating and wearing. He was empty now. There was nothing left to feel.

"What are you doing?" Nick lurched forward in his chair; his head snapped around to see who was behind him."Claire, what are you doing here?"

"I was just checking on you. Your door wasn't closed all the way, ya know." She sat down on the edge of his bed and clicked the back of her black high-heeled boots against the floor.

"You shouldn't be alone right now." Nick looked away from her and down at the letter. He folded it up and slid it into a black envelope.

"Who are you writing to?" she asked. She was always nosy, asking questions, listening in for gossip to spread around campus.

"It doesn't matter," Nick said, forcing a smile in her direction. Claire's dark eyes narrowed. She tucked her black hair behind her ears and leaned forward.

"You were writing a letter to him, weren't you?" His smile vanished, and he returned her piercing gaze, but he didn't answer.

"Well?"

"Yeah," he said. "It's weird, I know. Someone suggested I try it: write a letter to the dead. It's helping me get through it."

"It lets you say all the things you never got a chance to say," she said before he could continue. "I've never done it, but I can imagine its therapeutic implications. If only they could write us back."

He nodded his head and turned away from her. He stared out the window. The sky was darkening, and the sun barely peaked over the mountains in the distance.

"I miss him so much," he admitted, more to himself than to her. Immediately she was up again, and her hands were on his shoulders.

"I know, hun," she said. She kissed the top of his head. "I know it doesn't help to say, but we will all be missing him with you. We were all so close." She looked back at the second twin bed in the room. "It must be quiet in this little apartment without him."

"Sometimes I feel like he will burst into the room at any second," Nick said. "He'll jump on my bed yelling, 'Wake-up shots!'" Nick laughed. New liquid formed in the corners of his eyes.

"Have you gone to any of your classes this week?"

He shook his head. "I just … I can't focus. I'm losing it. Going out is a struggle; staying in this apartment where everything reminds me of him is a struggle." He looked around the studio apartment and exhaled loudly. The entire building served as off-campus housing for college students.

"You should get out of here," Claire said. "Come to the party tonight. You did get a costume, didn't you?"

"I don't think I'm up for it," he said.

"Come on, Nick, you know I'm not going to let you stay here alone tonight."

She hugged him from behind and kissed his neck. "We can all heal together," she whispered in his ear.

He knew she wasn't going to give him a choice. He'd either go to the party with her—or she would bring a party to him. "I'll meet you downstairs," he said quietly. "But I'm not staying out late."

"Meet me in two hours," she said, her voice revealing her excitement. "This is going to be so much fun!"

Nick spun around in his chair and watched her as she moved to the door. She turned back to face him.

"It will get easier," she said seriously.

He nodded his head. It didn't matter how many times people told him things like everything was going to be okay or that he would get through it. Those words never helped. Sure, they might have been right, but it didn't make it any easier. After Claire closed the door behind her, he got up and moved to the dark hallway leading past the tiny kitchen toward the bathroom. He hesitated as he neared the bathroom door. He could see light from the crack between the door and the floor. For a second, he thought he must have left the light on, but then he saw a slow-moving shadow ripple through the streak of light. He heard the creaky faucet handles turning and then water running.

"Claire?" he called.

But it couldn't have been Claire. She had left. He had watched her. After several seconds of listening to water running, he moved to the door and ripped it open. He paused as a sudden pain filled his sinuses and head. He clenched his eyes.

Blood. The walls, the white tile floor, and the bathtub were all smeared in red.

He slowly inhaled through his nose and out his mouth. He opened his eyes and glanced around the sterile bathroom. The blood was gone. That's where he'd found the body, sprawled out on the bathroom floor. He'd never be able to unsee it. Every time he walked into the room, he remembered all the blood.

A suicide, they'd determined. Nick knew the truth; he would have never killed himself. Even if it were possible, Nick didn't know which conclusion would have tormented him more: a suicide—or the alternative.

He noticed the water faucet was indeed running. He turned it off and looked at himself in the mirror. He hardly looked the same, as if he'd aged ten years in a few days. His brown eyes were tired, the skin around them dark and baggy. His curly black hair was matted, his skin dry. He hadn't showered in days. Claire must have noticed his musty smell but hadn't said anything. He stripped down and climbed into an almost scalding shower.

After thirty minutes, the water started to get cold, and he realized he'd probably used up the hot water on the whole floor. He stepped out the tub, dried his body, and wrapped the towel around his waist. He felt better now that he was clean, as if he had been able to scrub away some of the pain. He brushed his teeth in front of the foggy mirror. He wished he hadn't agreed to go out tonight. He didn't think he was ready, but Claire would only come back, and next time she'd be equipped with other friends.

He used his hand to clear the fog from the mirror. He could hardly see his face through the steam, but it wasn't just his face he saw. He almost choked on the foam in his mouth. He dropped the toothbrush and spun around.

There was nothing behind him. He turned back to the mirror, which had fogged up again. There had been a second face there; he knew it.

I'm going crazy, he thought. He'd been seeing things ever since his roommate's death, the day his life changed forever. He thought about going to see a counselor or a psychiatrist. A specialist from the school had reached out to him multiple times, but he hadn't called her back. He didn't want to talk to anyone about it. Talking about it only brought back memories.

Nick turned off the light and closed the door as he left the bathroom to return to his bedroom. He turned on the soundbar speaker mounted on his wall, lay out on his bed, and stared up at the ceiling while listening to Stateless' song, "I'm on Fire." He thought about curling up in bed and sleeping. He hadn't had a good night sleep in days. He rolled over onto his side and looked at the empty bed beside his. He couldn't imagine having another roommate, at least not this school year. That bed would remain empty for a long time.

Eventually, he forced himself up. The bag with his costume rested by his desk. He and his roommate had bought costumes together. Nick had planned to be Zeus, and his roommate had planned to be Osiris. Nick dumped the contents of the Osiris bag onto his bed. He lifted up the long black tunic and pulled it down over his head. He tied a gold belt around his waist and returned to the bathroom with his makeup kit. Nick stopped in the hallway when, once again, the light was on in the bathroom. This time, he knew he had turned it off.

Thick, red liquid began spewing out from under the door, as if the room was flooded with blood. He closed his eyes and tried to clear his mind.

"It's not real," he said aloud.

He heard the jiggling of the bathroom door handle, and his eyes opened wide. The blood was still flowing, and the door was slowly creaking open.

***

Claire opened her apartment door to find Nick standing there. It took her all of two seconds to assume that he was tweaking out. She looked at him with a mixture of empathy and pity.

"You're a little early," she said, standing in the doorway.

She looked gorgeous. Her long dark hair was curled. She wore a red jewel-encrusted crown and a poofy red and white dress with red heart shapes scattered about. She was the Queen of Hearts.

"I know, I just …" he sighed. "Claire, I think I'm going crazy. I've been …"

He struggled to find his words. "Never mind."

"Just come in, Nick," she said gently. "Have a seat with your friends. I'm almost ready."

When he entered the apartment, he spotted

Bruce and Tanya sitting on the couch. They held shot glasses to their mouths. They were dressed as Wendy and Peter Pan.

"Hey, Nick," Tanya called after making a disgusted face from the taste of the alcohol. "Want to take a shot?"

Nick shook his head.

Bruce stood up and put his arm around Nick. "I've missed you, buddy. It's been a while."

"I've missed you guys too," he said, turning from Bruce to Tanya, who had also stood up to hug him.

"How are you holding up?" she asked.

"Easier every day," Nick lied and shrugged. "I'll get through it."

"I could stay with you for a few nights if you want, man," Bruce said. "Keep you company."

"No, that's okay," Nick said. "Really. I couldn't stand the thought of you seeing me moping around the apartment." He forced a chuckle.

"That's why you have friends," Tanya said, "to put up with your moping."

"How about we all go to brunch tomorrow morning or something?" Nick suggested. "We can nurse our hangovers."

"Does that mean you've changed your mind about the shot?" Tanya asked, immediately lifting the bottle of vodka.

"I guess so," he said.

He took a swig straight from the bottle. He figured the booze would make him forget the things he saw—and forget that he was going crazy. They talked for several minutes about classes, tests, and parties they'd been to.

"Are we ready?" Claire asked, coming out of the hall-way. Her makeup was done to make her look pale, and she had red heart shapes painted on her cheeks. She did a twirl in her costume for their approval.

"Beautiful, as always," Tanya said, clasping her hands together.

Nick smiled but said nothing. He grabbed the bottle of vodka, lifted it up to his mouth, and took a long swig. Claire did some gold makeup and eyeliner for him before they left her apartment. Nick felt warm and fuzzy from his buzz by the time they got to the party. The aban-doned warehouse was lit up in black and neon lights. Nick took one look at the massive crowd and immediately regretted being there. But it beat sitting in his apartment alone, tripping out on his emotions.

"This is going to be awesome," Tanya said. "I can't believe how many people showed."

"Jesse texted me, saying she's up front by the DJ booth," Bruce said, more to Tanya than the rest of them. "It's gotta be so loud up there."

"Let's take another shot and then go up," Tanya said, smiling as she looked over at Nick.

Her smile slowly faded. Nick was staring forward in a trance-like state. Claire noticed Nick's vacant expression, too, and motioned with her head in the direc-tion of the bar.

"Get four tequila shots," she said.

She grabbed Nick's arm and pulled him toward the wall and away from people dancing.

"Nick, you've got to pull yourself together. We just got here, and you're already looking tragic."

"I'm trying," Nick snapped. "You are the one who dragged me out here."

"You aren't the only one who lost someone," she said, returning his bitter tone with one of her own. "So did I. We … we were all close Nick. As I'm sure he told you."

Nick narrowed his eyes at her.

"We were all close," her tone softened. "This is hard for all of us. We are all trying, and you need to try too. We are amongst friends. There are so many people here who care about you. He wouldn't want you to be like this."

"He's dead. Is it not okay to grieve?" Nick's voice was loud, yet no one around seemed to notice.

"Yes, it's okay to grieve. Of course it is," her voice returned to a tender tone. "But you can't stop living. You have to live on, for him." She kissed him on the cheek. "Now perk the fuck up and let's party!"

Nick forced a smile. "Tequila, huh?"

He put his arm around her waist, and they moved toward the bar.

"Always perks me up," she said.

By the time they forced their way through the crowd, Bruce and Tanya were holding plastic shot cups with salted limes.

"Happy Halloween, bitches!" Tanya screamed.

Nick did his best to appear happy as he danced with his friends, swaying his body to the beat of the base. The vibrations were a little overwhelming, as they stood so close to the stage. After the third tequila shot, he was feeling really good, like his head was lighter. His anxiety seemed to have lifted, and even if it was only momentary, he was grateful for the brief release.

Nick looked out at the smiling, drunken, rolling faces of the crowd of witches, zombies, vampires, and superheroes. He was happy he'd went with the Osiris outfit; he had only seen one other dressed similarly to him. His eyes stopped when he saw someone standing still in the rippling audience, staring back at him.

As Nick stared at him, it was as if everything around him slowed down: the music, the moving bodies. Everything was slow and fuzzy, except for the guy. He wasn't in costume. He was just wearing a white t-shirt and black shorts. Nick stopped moving. He couldn't pull his eyes away. He knew that what he saw was impossible. Nick smiled and took a step forward.

The man lifted his head to the ceiling, his throat opened up, and thick red liquid streamed down his neck and onto his shirt. Tanya turned away from her boyfriend and wrapped her arms around Nick's neck. That's when she noticed the horrified look on his face.

"Nick, are you okay?"

He closed his eyes and shook his head. Tears began

to drip from his eyes. Tanya glanced back at Claire and nodded toward the back door. Claire gave an awkward reassuring smile and continued to dance as Tanya pulled his arm and led him through the crowd toward the back of the room. There was a side door leading outside to an area where people smoked. She pushed the door open, and the burst of cool air felt good on his skin.

"I'm sorry," he said. "I lost it in there."

"It's okay," she said, pulling out a cigarette. She offered one to him, but he declined. "It was just probably a little too soon for you. But I'm proud of you for trying." She took a puff and exhaled away from him.

"It's just that …" His voice trailed off.

"You were in love with him," she said, as if it were obvious. Nick stared at her for a while before nodding his head.

"I guessed. Bruce owes me twenty dollars."

"Please don't tell him."

"You know no one cares, right? Come on now. We love you, always. Hell, I think I love you even more now."

She laughed. Nick didn't say anything.

"It's okay. Trust me, I understand. Men are hot."

They both laughed this time.

"He loved you too," Tanya said. "I saw it. Bruce saw it. Claire will deny it because she loved him too, but deep down, she knew it."

She chuckled lowly, more to herself than to Nick.

"Maybe you are the reason he broke up with her."

"Claire …"

"I knew it," she interrupted. "I can tell just by the look on your face. You stole her man."

"It wasn't like that. They stayed friends afterward."

"You and I both know they only stayed friends because Claire wanted him back. They still spent way too much time together, if you ask me."

"I didn't ask you," he snapped. Then he quickly shook his head. "Sorry. It was hard. Everything was hard, getting him to admit it, getting him to open up to me about it, and she was always there. That didn't make it any easier."

"I understand," Tanya said. "But don't say anything about it to Claire," she warned, turning serious. "Claire took it really hard, both the breakup and his death. She's tough, though, or pretends to be. It's just better if we keep this all between us. You both will get through it."

"I don't know what to do."

"Start by taking some new guy home with you tonight," she said after taking another drag of her cigarette.

He laughed, "No way! It's a little too soon for that."

"Well, promise me that you will come out already to everyone. You know I can't keep secrets."

"Yet I'm supposed to trust you not to tell Claire that I stole her boyfriend?"

"That's different." she said. "A few secrets are worth keeping. I just don't want to see any more misery. So, you can trust me."

"I know I can." he said. "Tomorrow, at brunch, I'll tell them about me."

"Bruce can stay with you tonight if you want, keep you company. But don't get any ideas."

"I'd never do that," he laughed. "But really, I'm okay. I kind of want to be alone tonight anyway. I think I've reached being-around-people overload at this point."

"You want to go home now?"

"Not yet. You go ahead and go back in; I'll be in in a bit. I know where to find you guys."

She crossed her arms over her chest.

"I'm not leaving yet; I'm just going to enjoy the cool air a bit longer."

"Okay," she said. "Five minutes." She made a motion with her fingers, letting him know that she was watching him, and then turned to go back inside.

Nick sighed and leaned back against the brick wall and slumped down until his butt was practically on his heels. There were twenty or thirty other people outside smoking. He glanced around at all of them, careful not to lock eyes with anyone. He wasn't particularly in the mood to talk to random people. He closed his eyes and put his head down on his lap. He felt a little better after talking to Tanya; she always seemed to know just what to say, and he liked her "I have zero fucks to give" attitude.

"Hey," Nick heard a voice above him. He looked up to find a guy he recognized. The guy was wearing a red tunic and a thin gold leaf headband, and he held out a cigarette. "You okay, Nick?"

"Yeah, I'm fine." This time, Nick took the cigarette. The man was tall with broad shoulders, dark eyes, and even darker skin.

"You've been down there quite a while," he said. It wasn't until those words hit him that Nick realized that his left foot was asleep. The guy reached out his hand and helped Nick to his feet. He had lightning bolt stickers on his arms.

"Thanks, Quintin," Nick said. He suddenly felt light-headed and stumbled a bit before leaning back against the wall.

"Woah, easy there." Quintin held out a light for Nick's cigarette. "Who'd you come with?"

"Claire, Tanya, and Bruce. But I don't feel like going back in there to find them." Nick took a drag. "But I'll be fine. I'm just going to walk home."

"This wasn't really my scene either," Quintin said. "I'd take a horror movie night with good beer or visiting haunted places over a Halloween party any year."

"I have horror movies and beer at the apartment," Nick said.

"I don't know if you need any more beer."

"I didn't mean for me. I'd probably just smoke a joint or something."

"That I could probably go for," Quintin said.

Nick texted Tanya that he decided to go home after all, with a side note to please not be angry with him. The two guys made their way from the party and down the road toward the dorms. Nick felt his sense of balance return after he started walking again. He thought of Claire and how disappointed she would pretend to be that he left. He figured with his behavior, he'd probably succeeded in making her regret dragging him out in the first place. Still, he felt bad for not saying goodbye to them.

"Here we are," Nick said, stopping for a second in front of the brown brick building. He remembered the blood in the bathroom.

"Keep it together," he said quietly aloud.

"Huh?" Quintin asked.

"Oh, nothing," Nick said, forcing a smile. "So, what's your favorite horror movie?"

When the guys entered the apartment, Nick threw off his crown.

"I'm going to scrub this stuff off my face first," he said.

Quintin nodded, moved to the fridge, and grabbed a beer. Nick hesitated in the hallway in front of the bathroom door. The door was wide open, despite him knowing he closed it, but there didn't appear to be blood everywhere like before.

He took a cautious step into the room and closed the door. He stared at himself in the mirror. His eyes were pink and puffy. He ran the water until it was warm and lifted his black polyester robe up and over his head. He soaked his face and scrubbed at his skin with a towel. When he finished, he dropped the towel on the floor. He looked exhausted. He stared at himself for awhile, his eyes locked on his own. He didn't blink, didn't move, didn't breathe.

There was something off about his reflection. Something he saw inside of himself. A sad, lonely darkness, but also anger. Suddenly, the reflection in the mirror moved, and Nick jumped back and almost fell into the bathtub. His reflection didn't jump back. Instead his reflection lifted his hand, which clutched a knife, and he drug the blade across his throat. Blood gushed from the open wound. Nick closed his eyes, sunk to the floor, and sobbed. He knew it; he was crazy. He had completely lost himself in his grief.

When he opened his eyes, he stared at himself again—his normal pathetic self. He sighed and turned toward the door, but he stopped once his hand gripped the handle. It couldn't be. He turned back to the sink and picked up the knife that was resting on the back edge by his toothbrush. He flung it in the cabinet below the sink, but he didn't hear a clank. He glanced around the shelves, but there was no knife. He'd imagined it, the same way he must have been hallucinating all night.

He fled the bathroom. Part of him wanted to crawl into bed and hide from the world, but the other part of him was grateful for the company, anything to distract him from what was happening in his mind. He forced himself to try not to look like he was freaking out. Quintin was relaxing on Nick's bed, his gold sandals still on. He was holding up two movies.

"'The Witch' or 'It Follows'? I've heard great things about both."

"That's because both are amazing," Nick said, his voice shaking despite his effort to maintain his composure. "Two of the best horror movies I've seen in a long time."

He knew he wouldn't make it through a single movie; he'd pass out as soon as he lay down.

"Are you okay?" Quintin asked. "Are you sure you want to stay up? I can let you sleep instead."

"No!" Nick said, a little too loudly. "I mean, I'm fine. Let's just smoke a bowl."

Quintin took a swig of his beer, "Light it up, man."

Nick moved over to his desk and looked down at the letter he'd written earlier. He could have sworn he put it away, but it was sitting there, unfolded and ready to read. He pulled open one of the drawers to grab his pipe. He loaded it with pot, took his lighter, and climbed into bed beside Quintin.

"Nick," Quintin started, "There's something that I want to talk to you about."

"But first," Nick cut him off and held out the pipe to him. "Let's smoke a little."

Quintin smiled and took the pipe from him. He lit the bowl and took a long puff.

"If this is a serious talk, can we have it tomorrow?" Nick asked. "I'm probably hardly going to remember it anyway. I'm so messed up."

Quintin coughed and passed the pipe. He hesitated before answering with a nod. Nick smoked a little, then lay down beside Quintin and rested his head on his shoulder.

"I should let you sleep," Quintin said.

"Don't leave," Nick said, his head already cloudy. He was so tired.

He felt Quintin shift, but he didn't leave. Instead, he lay flat and held Nick to him. Nick was asleep in less than a minute. Quintin lay there for an hour or so, unable to sleep. Eventually, he gently repositioned Nick on the bed and got up to turn off the bedroom light. Then he moved to the hallway leading to the bathroom. He opened the bathroom door and fumbled for the light. He flipped the switch, and the ceiling light flickered for several seconds before making a loud buzzing sound as it burned out.

He glanced back down the empty hallway. Barely any light shone through the windows of the bedroom. If he closed the door, he would be in total darkness. He moved deeper into the dark bathroom toward the toilet that he couldn't even see. He reached down for it to feel for the seat. He heard a creak of weight on the wooden floor from outside the bathroom and turned his head. Someone was standing there. In the hallway. Staring at him.

"Nick?" he called. "Turn on the light, man. This one in the bathroom is out."

The shadowy figure in the hallway didn't move.

"Nick?" Quintin stood there for a moment, staring into the dark hallway.

The shadowy figure took two steps forward. The hair on the back of his neck stiffened and—in an instant—he knew what was going to happen. Quintin moved to slam the door, but he was already too late. As he outstretched his arm toward the door, he felt a sharp pain in his wrist.

He yanked his arm back and clenched his right hand over the deep gash on his arm from the knife wound. He stumbled back against the wall as the shadow moved into the room and slammed the door, sealing them in darkness.

The next afternoon, Claire quickly walked down the hallway toward Nick's apartment. She raised her fist to knock on the door, but before her fist hit the wood, the doorknob turned and opened a crack. She stood there for a moment, waiting for the door to further open. It didn't. She pushed the door all the way open and found no one on the other end.

"Nick!" she called, taking a step inside.

She closed the door behind her and glanced around the room. He wasn't in bed, at his desk, or standing in the kitchen. She saw a light on under the bathroom door down the hallway and assumed he was in there.

"Nick, you missed brunch!" she called loudly. "Which was your idea, by the way."

She didn't hear a reply, but she was sure she heard water running. She moved over toward his desk to sit and wait for him to get out.

She looked down at the piece of paper sitting on the desk. She didn't want to invade his privacy, but she couldn't help but read the first sentence. She reached down and picked it up. She realized there were two papers, one on top of the other. She briefly glanced at the bottom letter but focused on reading the top one.

She lifted the letter until it was so close to her face she could barely read it. Her hand was shaking. The letter still sitting on the table was written by Nick to Quintin: the letter she had seen Nick writing the night before. The letter in her hand was a letter from Quintin to Nick. The first sentence of the letter in her hand read,

Nick, there's something I want to talk to you about.

The two letters were written in different handwriting, which should have been impossible. Quintin was dead. The letter must have been written before he died, but—somehow—she knew it wasn't. The letter was written after last night, and it referred to things that Nick shouldn't have known, things about what she and Quintin did two weeks ago while Nick was back home, just days before he died. It was an apology letter.

She gritted her teeth as she read on. She felt the familiar sting of betrayal. She wanted to tear the letter in half. She heard the bathroom door slam. She spun around to face Nick, standing across the room. He was shirtless and wearing a red towel around his waist. He stared at her, his eyes full of fury. She stared back at him, her eyes every bit as deranged and angry. They stood there, glaring at each other for a long time before one of them finally spoke.

"You killed him."

HELPING HANDS

"Why won't you just let me in?" I asked, equal parts sympathetic and frustrated.

Gene sat in nothing but his gym shorts, on his bare, worn-down mattress. His head hung low; he was avoiding my eyes.

"Will you please open up to me?" I leaned down and spoke softly in his ear. "You don't have to endure your burdens alone." He didn't say anything. I placed a tender hand on his head and brushed his matted brown hair. It was damp from sweat.

"All you have to do is let me in," I said, smiling.

I kissed his forehead.

"Stop … just stop." That was all he said. He didn't

look up; he just kept staring down at the hardwood floor. There was an empty handle of whiskey on the floor.

"I'll give you some time alone. You can think things over," I said.

I moved my hand from his head to his chin and lifted it until his burgundy eyes met mine. I could see the emptiness hidden behind them, a darkness that matched the black veil that surrounded him. He looked so defeated.

"I'll see you tomorrow, okay?"

He turned his eyes from me to the empty pale yellow walls. I sighed and turned to move toward the door, but he suddenly grabbed my wrist. The grip was rough, aggressive. He still wasn't looking at me. His fingers loosened, and the embrace became sincere, even pleading.

"You don't have to leave," he said, almost too quiet for me to hear.

"I just think you need some time." I stopped talking as he pulled me down onto the bed with him.

He didn't say another word. I didn't say another word. I just let him hold me tightly to him for a while in silence. He clutched me with both arms, his fingers gently caressing my back. *You don't want to open up, yet you don't want to be alone. How do I help you?* We lay there, listening to the rain outside for at least an hour, before he finally fell asleep. I slithered out of his arms, and his eyes opened a crack. I kissed him on the neck before getting up to leave.

I stopped in front of the door.

"I really do love you, Gene."

"I know. I love you, too, Alex," he said quietly. "No one has ever been as kind to me as you are."

Once outside, I walked down the sidewalk toward the busier part of downtown. It was still raining softly and the cool water felt nice on my face. As I walked the busy streets, I took note of everyone I saw. As people passed, I examined their feelings and their mental stability. It's always surprising and disheartening to see just how many people are lonely, broken.

I can sense it on them, shades of grey, and the faintest smell of burnt flesh. I was looking for someone surrounded by total blackness. The utterly helpless one, like I was once. To exist was to be cuffed down to a nail-covered chair in the great torture chamber of the universe, awaiting what surprise horrors the bitch called Life planned to inflict on you next. Sure, there were enjoyments, those brief reprieves in between hammer strokes on your fingers, but for many of us, they are few and far between.

I tried not to think about what my life had been like. I looked at my past in the mirror, and I shattered it with a sledgehammer. Sometimes shards of memory cut through my brain to the surface of my skull, but they were easy enough to pluck out and cast aside. I had learned to overcome my pain, and now I helped others overcome theirs. Some people stood there on the streets, asking for donations to save rainforests or to provide medication for babies in other countries. I wandered the streets attempting to save the broken, the depressed.

The best part is, I didn't want your money. I only wanted you.

It was taking a lot longer than I had hoped to save Gene. For the past three months, I had seen him almost every day, and spent most of my nights at his apartment. Our first encounter was just outside a bar in an alley. He had a few too many tequila shots, a liquor that seemed to stimulate his anger more than it did for others. He had pissed off a couple of smaller guys, and they had decided they were going to jump him.

Gene was drunk, but he was a well-built man, and none of the cowards dared approach him alone. The guys followed him out of the bar. After they took turns punching and kicking him, I was right there, ready to comfort him.

"Why are you helping me?" he asked, unable to walk straight, even with my help.

"Because I'm your guardian angel," I said with a laugh. "And I'm here to change your life."

From that night on, I was his best friend, his only real friend. My presence alone helped dull the sharp emptiness I knew he felt inside. Tomorrow I would be much more persistent with him, I decided. Where much was given, much was expected, and I was expected to do great things.

Two small children in bright raincoats ran past me, giggling, and their mother struggled to keep up. Children, I don't know what it is about them, but they shine so brightly. Yellows, golds, and bright oranges seem to encompass them. It's for that reason I can never touch them. Maybe when they get older and they witness the ruthless brutality of the world, maybe then I'll be able to save them. *Stay young and happy forever, kids. Don't ever grow up. Growing up sucks.*

It hadn't been long since I was saved myself. HE came for me when I was alone. I don't mean physically alone, but really, truly alone. The kind of alone where if someone looked into your eyes they'd see a vacancy sign because even you had abandoned your own suit of meat.

That was the loneliness that attracted HIM. HE saw me, hollowed out by the trials of life, and filled my empty vessel with a new being. HE gave me love, HE gave me companionship, and finally, a purpose. A part of HIM lived inside of me, and now I am never alone.

I remembered our first meeting. I was sitting against the wall in an abandoned warehouse, alone. People occasionally threw raves there that I always avoided, but on normal nights, no one ventured there, other than the occasional homeless person, or guys looking to make a deal. I held the empty needle in my hand and waited for the colors and serenities to wash over me.

The feeling soon came, but it wasn't as intense as the previous time. Instead, I found myself struggling to move more than usual. My body felt as if it weighed a thousand pounds. I heard laughter in the distance. Through my blurring vision, I saw three men approaching; one I recognized as Jackal, my dealer. The other two I had seen before, but couldn't recall their names. I remembered their twisted smiles and wild, hungry eyes as the three of them stood over me. I probably should have been afraid, yet I found myself feeling nothing at all.

"Looks like Alex is having a really nice trip," one of Jackal's friends said as they closed in on me. He was tall and thin, and the skin on his face was dry and cracked.

"Probably flew all the way to the moon."

"Don't worry, Alex," Jackal said, kneeling down until he was right in front of my face. "We'll look out for you."

"We will take good care of you," his friend spoke again.

Jackal's hand moved to his crotch, and he fumbled with his zipper. The third guy wasn't paying attention; he was looking back behind them. I closed my eyes and waited. I knew what was coming. This hadn't been the first time Jackal had done this.

I wasn't only addicted to his top-quality treats I frequently injected myself with, I let him needle me the same way. Our relationship was beyond fucked up. I enjoyed him the way a gazelle enjoyed being torn apart and eaten by lions … oh wait, it doesn't enjoy being mutilated, so why did I? Why did I run right into his jaws over and over and over again, knowing exactly what his teeth felt like on my neck?

I waited. But nothing happened. Everything was suddenly quiet. I struggled to reopen my eyes, but when I did, the men were gone and I was alone again. I wondered if I had imagined the whole thing.

That's when I saw HIM. HE slowly walked over to

me and smiled, a smile that seemed to warm my whole body. I had never seen a more beautiful person in my entire life. Even in the darkness, I could see HIS pale eyes. They almost glowed.

"I'm here now," HE said in a deep and soothing voice. "I won't let them hurt you again."

HE sat down beside me and put a strong arm around my shoulders. The gesture was unexpected. I could hardly move, let alone pull away, and I found myself oddly comfortable. HIS touch was so tender. I found myself nuzzling my head in HIS neck, and I drifted back off into the void of my mind.

I'm not sure how long I slept there in HIS arms, but while I slept, I think HE was there with me in my dreams. When I awoke, I was no longer in the abandoned warehouse, but in an almost offensively white room. Everything from the walls, to the furniture, to the carpet was the same shade of bright white. I sat up quickly, somehow more afraid of waking up in this unknown room than I was with Jackal and his friends.

"Where am I?"

"Shhh, it's okay." I heard HIS calming voice.

HE was sitting in a chair at a desk across the room. HE wore black slacks and a matching vest over a red T-shirt. HE looked a bit older than me, in his early thirties.

"I was wondering when you were going to wake up."

HE smiled at me, and instantly all of my fears were gone. Every fiber of his being radiated a mixture of strength, authority, and most of all, love.

"This place," he motioned to the room around him. "It's heaven." HE chuckled. "Or maybe it's just my home."

"Who are you?" I asked.

I couldn't help but smile at HIM. HE held an irresistibly alluring presence, almost divine.

"I'm whoever you want or need me to be," HE said, standing up. HE reached out his hand to me.

A blaring car horn brought me back from my daydream as several jaywalkers ran across the street. The memories I enjoyed with HIM were so vivid, it was as if I could relive them in my mind. I watched as the jaywalkers passed a building, and in front of that building was where I saw HIM standing, waving at me. HE always knew where to find me.

A tall and beautiful black woman stood beside him. Her long, shiny-bright brown hair was lighter than her dark skin, and even from across the street, I could see her almost golden eyes. She wore a tight black dress that must have been made for her body. Their arms were linked. HE was holding a white umbrella over their heads.

I hurried across the street and smiled eagerly. "I was just thinking about you."

"Come on," HE said, motioning for me to follow them into the building.

Above the double doors was a sign that said Helping Hands in golden letters that formed an arch. The woman eyed me. She seemed intrigued. The building was filled with offices, each with walls and doors of glass. I followed HIM toward the back. HE unlocked a large white door and motioned for the woman and me to enter. The room was just as bright as the room that I awoke in when I had first spoken to HIM, and it was the only room that didn't have walls of glass.

"Have a seat, Alex," HE said, grinning.

HE pulled out a chair for me. Before I sat down, HE pulled me to him and held me tightly. HE kissed me on the forehead. As I tried to pull away, HE kissed me very quickly on the mouth. HE then pulled out another chair for the woman.

"I'd like to introduce you to Morgan." I reached out my hand to shake.

"We don't shake hands here," she said, almost laughing.

"I'm sorry." My awkward smile matched my tone. "I'm still getting used to … everything."

This time she did laugh, and then tossed back her hair, hugged me, and kissed me on the mouth. The embrace felt nice, and I found myself disappointed that the kiss didn't last longer.

"You are adorable," she said, tucking a strand of hair behind my ear. We both sat next to each other at the large rectangular table. HE sat across from us.

"What is this place?" I asked.

"This place actually belongs to me," Morgan said, crossing her legs. "It's a clinical social work agency that I own. It is family run. We specialize in helping those who suffer from depression and bipolar disorder. We also offer a lot of grief counseling." She smiled proudly. "It's just my way of giving back to the community."

"You must have a big family," I said.

"Growing every day," she said. "We are everywhere. And you are the newest member of HIS family," she said. "It's not so often that HE personally saves someone. It's an honor being a part of HIS immediate family. A firstborn. HE saved me too, long ago."

"She was the first of my progeny," HE said, nodding, leaning all the way back in the chair. "And since then she has brought so many into the fold, saved countless lives."

HIS praise seemed to lift her to the ceiling. I only hoped that one day HE would speak about me in such a glorious manner.

"Have you started building a family of your own?" she asked.

"Yes, what progress have you made with saving Gene?" HE asked.

"We are close," I said. "Ever since the night we met, we have been seeing each other almost every day. He says he loves me."

He'd said it a few times, but there was something missing in his voice. His words were like the sparks intended to light a fire, but to no avail, as there was too much wind.

"I'm a little disappointed," HE said.

The words cut me, and I suddenly felt as if I was bleeding out from my wrists. HE'd never expressed any negativity toward me before.

"I had surely thought Gene would have been an easy person for you to save," HE continued. "I do hope you make more progress soon. I hope I wasn't wrong about you. You seemed to show such promise."

"I will bring him into my family," I said, trying to sound more confident and determined. "Forgive me. I didn't mean to disappoint you. I am going to see him again tomorrow."

"Why not tonight?" HE asked. "Stay the night with him. Stay with him. Stay true to him, and he will find himself stronger in your presence."

"I'm sure you will succeed," Morgan said, patting me on the shoulder. "Remember, you are doing this for Gene. His happiness depends on you. If you truly love him, you can't let him down."

I knocked on Gene's apartment door and waited, resisting the urge to unlock the door and walk in myself. I waited for nearly an entire minute before he opened the door. He looked almost overly happy to see me.

"I'm so glad you are actually smiling," I said, hugging him. He closed the door behind me. His normal black aura was now a few shades lighter, a dark gray.

"Well, I have something I have to tell you."

The eagerness and excitement showed a side of him I hadn't seen in a while.

"Have you made your choice? Have you decided to come with me?"

"I don't think that's necessary anymore," he said.

My body felt unexpectedly heavy, and I could feel IT suddenly crawling around inside of my belly.

"She called me today," he said, smiling wider now. "She says she needs to talk to me. It's been almost a year since I've seen her. She is coming over soon. I want you to meet her."

"Lisa?"

"Yes, of course; who else?"

"Why are you talking to her again?" I asked, my tone a lot angrier than I meant it to sound.

I'm not sure where the anger was coming from. Perhaps I was so angry for Gene's sake. I wanted so desperately to help him, and he was ruining it by talking to some bitch who had left him a shriveled heap. He was choosing her over me. Gene's smile lessened, but didn't disappear.

"I thought you would be happy for me, Alex. That's what friends are supposed to be."

"I'm more than just your friend, Gene," I said, touching his face with my hand. "I love you too much to watch you let yourself be hurt by her again. She is only going to use you like she did last time, to build you up just so that she can shatter you again. You said it yourself when I first met you."

"It's …" he paused, his smile was completely

gone now. "It's complicated." He sat down on his mattress. "It wasn't just her. It was me, too. The night she left …" He stopped again, seeming to replay the moment in his mind, "I really scared her. I almost … I almost hit her. She just made me so crazy sometimes. Have you ever been in love?"

"I'm in love with you," I said gently.

Gene half-smiled, then lowered his gaze so that his eyes no longer met mine.

"It wasn't a healthy relationship between you two. You need to understand that. Going back to the past will only doom you to repeat it. Don't do this. Just let me save you. There is still time, before you allow yourself to go through this cycle again. Choose me, Gene. I am your light. I can show you the way to true happiness."

His face filtered through several emotions in a row, and then finally settled on something that must have been grief.

"I just don't know what to do, Alex. Just let me see her." He looked at me pleadingly, as if he needed my permission. "Just let me talk to her. I just want the closure."

"You will let me in!" I yelled, enraged.

The rage took even me by surprise. The voice I spoke with wasn't one that I recognized. It was much too deep. The lights flickered when I yelled, and in the milliseconds of darkness, I saw my eyes in the mirror across the room. Only they weren't their normal brown color. Instead, they glowed a deep, dark red.

Gene scooted back across the mattress until his back was against the wall. He was breathing heavily. I could feel his heart pounding, hear the blood rushing through his veins.

"I'm sorry," I said, shaking away my anger. I suddenly felt awful for having scared him. "I just don't want to see you hurting anymore." I turned and quickly walked back to the door. "I won't wait until she comes and pretend that I'm okay with this. I'll just go."

Gene didn't say anything as I left, but I could feel his still-frightened eyes on my back. As soon as I exited the building, my cell phone rang. I already knew who it was; only one person ever called me.

"What happened, Lex?" HE asked.

"Lisa happened," I snapped. "She is what is standing in the way of Gene's happiness. He won't come with me."

"Of course he will."

"I don't understand," I said, frustrated, "I don't understand why it's so hard for me to do this. I mean, you had no trouble saving me."

It had taken HIM a little over a week. When I wasn't taking care of my mother, I was always with HIM. HE kept me off heroin the entire time. I remembered the day I decided to go with HIM. I had cried a lot that day because my mother had finally succumbed to her illness. I had found her that morning in her bed. She looked so peaceful. The death came as a shock to me, because I thought she had been doing better. She had started to get back into her daily routine. She was leaving the house again, visiting her friends, going shopping and to church.

HE came over as soon as I called. After my mother's body was taken, HE took me on a long drive to the mountains. HE held my hand almost the entire drive. We hiked for a few hours, and then stopped to rest and ate sandwiches when we made it to the top of the cliff.

"I'm really sorry about your mother," HE said for the tenth time that day.

"I thought things were getting better," I said, looking out at the mountains and trees that stretched as far as I could see. "I thought she might be okay. Now even she left me."

"She had to," HE said. "It was her time."

"People always leave."

"I won't," HE said, putting his arm around my shoulders. "I'll never leave you. Not if you don't want me to."

"Of course I don't want you to. I'm not sure why you stay with me, though. I mean, look at you, you're perfect. And look at me. I'm just some pathetic, weakling addict."

"You don't see what I see," HE said, turning my gaze to meet HIS intense eyes.

"I don't look on the surface. I only look at what is inside." HE placed his hand on my chest above my heart. "Through me, what is weak can become strong. What is broken can become whole again. I will be your lover, your brother, your father, and your God. You can be with me forever. All you have to do is let me in."

I nodded, "I want to be with you forever."

HE kissed me. The kiss lasted a long time, and

something crawled up from inside of HIM and entered me. IT was rubbery, scaly, and slimy all at the same time, yet IT tasted so sweet. IT slithered down my throat. IT filled me with intense warmth, and I felt HIS love inside of me, radiating through me.

"Saving people takes practice," HE said to me over the phone. "There have been several of my children who have saved so many people at once. Everyone uses a different approach. You will perfect your own way of saving people. Now, save Gene. You truly love him, don't you?"

"Of course I do. He's wonderful."

"Then you will do whatever it takes. His happiness depends on you."

"I will. I love you."

"I love you more," HE said, and then hung up.

When Lisa opened the door of her apartment to see who knocked on the door, she was surprised to find me standing there.

"Oh," she said, eyes wide. "Can I help you?"

She half smiled. She was moderately pretty, thin, pale, blonde. I didn't understand how Gene could be so infatuated with her. I could feel IT again, scratching from within my chest. IT wanted her, but not in the same way that IT wanted Gene.

"You will never hurt him again!" I grabbed the back

of her head and forced her mouth to mine.

A piece of IT climbed up my esophagus, clawed its way into her mouth, and invaded her body. She stumbled backward and dropped to her knees. I took a step into her apartment, and the door slammed behind me. She sat there confused and in pain, frightened, coughing, gagging. She fell flat onto her back. I stood and watched as she clutched her stomach.

"Please ..." was all she could say.

I had never seen a more frightened, pathetic expression. I wondered what IT was doing to her in there. She rolled over onto her stomach and half-crawled, half-dragged herself across the floor toward the back room of the apartment. She continued to cough, tried to scream but couldn't. Blood dripped from her mouth, and she choked on it.

"Please don't hurt ..." She stopped and lay flat, motionless.

A few seconds later, her heart stopped. I sat on her soft couch and grabbed her half-empty glass of white wine on the coffee table. I sipped her peachy Moscato and watched as her corpse began to move. She got up, moved to the kitchen table, and pulled her cell phone out of her bag. She called Gene.

After she broke his heart once again, she put the phone back into her purse and lay back on the floor, still. I rose and walked over to her body. I knelt and touched her lips with mine once again. IT ripped its way back up her through her esophagus, slithered back into my mouth and down into my body.

Without hesitating, I walked back toward the front door, but froze when I heard the cry. A soft cry from the back room. I shivered. I turned and cautiously approached the door to the bedroom. Once I opened the door, I could see the wooden crib beside the bed. I could see the eerie yellow glow emanating from it before I was close enough to see the baby lying there. His eyes and mouth were wide with fear as his crying grew louder.

Frozen, I stared at the baby. Pure, helpless, fragile, motherless. IT wiggled around inside me. The longer I stood there, the faster IT moved, until there was a sharp pain in the pit of my stomach. IT wanted me to leave. The baby had Gene's eyes. I clenched my fists so tightly that my nails dug into the flesh of my palms.

"I'm so sorry," I choked.

I dropped to my knees from the sudden intense pain in my belly, and crawled backward until my back was against the wall. I sat there, breathing heavily, holding my gut. The distance between the baby and me seemed to calm IT within me. The baby's crying turned shrill, desperate.

"I can't help you," I said, my eyes suddenly wet. "I can't touch you."

I sat there for what must have been an hour, until the baby had cried himself back to sleep. When all was silent, I stood up and left. I left the front door of the apartment wide open. I hoped someone would find the body and the child soon.

The next morning, I went back over to Gene's place, an hour before he was supposed to go to work. This time I had to let myself in. I found him in bed, staring up at the ceiling.

"Morning," I called, trying to sound cheerful. "I'm really sorry that I got so angry last night."

"You were right," he said, not looking at me. "I actually thought things were getting better. She sounded so happy to talk to me, like she really needed me, you know. But I guess I was wrong. I'm sorry I doubted you. Lisa really is a bitch."

"She will never love you as much as I do," I said, sitting beside him. I brushed my hand through his hair.

"I know that now," he said, looking over at me. He placed his big hand on my leg and squeezed.

"I'm sorry. I can't believe I was going to throw everything that we have away over her." He smiled at me. "No one has ever treated me as kindly as you have. You always go out of your way to try and make me happy."

He grabbed my hand and pulled me to him. I relaxed in his arms, my head on his chest.

"I don't deserve you. Do you forgive me?"

"You don't even have to ask," I said. I kissed him. "Are you ready to let me in?"

"I am," he said.

I kissed him again, and this time, when a piece of IT broke off and slithered down his throat, it took residence there, and filled him with my love, and HIS love. Without a word, Gene stood up and moved to the kitchen. He pulled open one of the drawers, and pulled out the biggest kitchen knife he had. He walked back toward me, the biggest smile on his face. He stopped and gripped the knife tightly in his hand.

"I'll see you soon," I said.

"I love you," he said, and for the first time I knew he meant it.

"I love you more."

He raised the knife and slid the blade across his throat with such determination that he hit his spinal cord.

I left the apartment. It would take a few days for him to return to me, reborn. I walked back to Helping Hands. I knew I would find HIM there. I thought back to the day in the mountains when I was saved. I'd so willingly jumped from that cliff, my body breaking against the rocks below. I felt no pain, only joy. Gene's joy … as he died for me, it gave me hope. Hope that I could forgive myself for what I had done because he would always carry that joy with him.

"Congratulations," HE said when I entered the white office. HE opened HIS arms wide, as if to hug me from afar. HE sat in the same chair. HIS black shirt was unbuttoned.

"I'm so proud of you," Morgan said. She was sitting cross-legged on the table. "The first member of your family. How does it feel?"

"Honestly, not as satisfying as I thought it would be," I said, standing in the center of the room.

My arms were crossed protectively over my chest. She frowned for less than a second before her face was cheerful again.

"Morgan, my love, will you give Alex and I a minute?"

"Of course, darling," she said, standing up. She placed a gentle, reassuring hand on my shoulder as she walked past.

"What's the matter, Alex?" HE asked with genuine concern. HE motioned for me to sit down in his lap.

"I …" I paused.

I remembered something that Gene had said, something very similar to something I had said to HIM the day that HE saved me.

"I did something horrible. I killed someone. A mother." My voice was low, shaking. "I didn't think I was capable of something like that."

"We are all capable of doing things we thought we might never do."

"Saving Gene didn't feel right. I thought I was doing something good."

"Gene is going to wake up feeling better than he ever has. He is going to love you, and he is going to be with you forever. He will be a part of your family, and he will have the opportunity to start a family of his own. Does that not sound like a good thing?"

"He already had a family!" I said loudly. "A son."

"Gene was in no shape to be a father. But he will be now. Through you and your love and devotion, he has become strong again. Now he will have many children."

"When I first saw you, I thought you were an angel. I thought I was an angel. I thought that I was some divine being meant to save others. Now I know. I'm not an angel. I'm a demon."

HIS eyes narrowed at me, and for a second, I thought HE might actually be angry with me.

"Demons are angels, too."

"Did you kill my mother?"

HIS anger evaporated. HE stared at me for a while, HIS face not showing a trace of emotion.

"You didn't need to carry that burden. I was helping you, freeing you. There couldn't be anything holding you back. You did want to be with me, didn't you?"

"You …" I couldn't finish.

I couldn't find my words. Instead, I slowly walked around the table. I stood over HIM, my hands clenched into fists. HE looked up at me with an apologetic smile. IT soothingly slithered around in my belly. I knew I should be furious, yet I found myself unable to stay mad at HIM. I truly loved HIM more than I had ever loved anyone. I slowly unclenched my fists .

"Everything I did, I did for you," HE said.

I nodded and then kissed him on the forehead. I turned away from him and moved toward the door.

"Where are you going? Morgan and I want to take

you to a celebration. I want to show you off to all my other children. You are my sparkling, new gem."

"I just want to be alone for a while."

"You are never alone anymore," HE said. "I'm always with you. I'm always inside you."

"I know," I said, placing a hand on the doorknob, but I didn't turn it.

"It gets easier," HE said. "It gets better. There are so many joys that we are going to share together. You have only had a taste of what is to come. Now that you have proven yourself, you will receive your wings, and then all things will be made clear to you." HE stood up and outstretched HIS arms. "You and I are forever. I love you."

"I love you more," I said and smiled.

I removed my hand from the doorknob and walked towards HIM. I suddenly longed for HIS touch, HIS eternal embrace. I could feel the warmth of HIS love inside of me.

LILLY'S LOVE

I kissed the soft head of the little white rat and gently stroked the fur of his belly with my finger.

"Fear not, darling," I whispered in his ear. He wriggled his nose at me. "For the pain is ours, little one."

The wooden cage was narrow, but tall, and fit perfectly in the corner of the room. I placed the rodent in the cage, closed the sliding glass door, and took a step back. The rat pawed at the dark bark bedding and moved to explore his new home. It stopped and placed its tiny front paws on the glass and stared at me.

Lamia didn't hesitate. The red snake lowered her head from the makeshift tree branch and sunk her fangs into his soft flesh. I listened intently to the rat's high-pitched squeal of pain, and my entire body quivered. I felt for the creature.

I understood him. I, too, am a mouse who has lain with vipers, offered up my soft, fuzzy warmth to their cold, rough bodies.

Strike me. Squeeze me. Please me. For who doesn't long for a love that devours? Lamia pulled the squirming rodent up to the branch and wrapped it in a tight cocoon of scales. I found myself gently touching my throat. It hadn't been long since I had experienced a similar embrace.

"Open the door, you bitch!" I could still hear my husband's voice outside the bathroom door, the pounding of his fists on the wood. I had thought the door might break, or that he'd kick it down. Eventually, I had to let him in. I moved from the snake cage to my bed, to tidy the sheets.

My husband liked a neat bed … or was it me who liked a neat bed? He was always so clean and organized when I met him, and I just assumed that he liked the bed to be made. I heard footsteps coming up the stairs as I smoothed out the comforter, and tucked it under the white pillows. My friend and colleague Juvia was half an hour early today.

"It's not his fault," I told Juvia as I examined my face in the bathroom mirror.

It took longer to do my makeup today. Darker colors were needed, along with multiple layers. The wine-purple blush worked surprisingly well with my pale complexion. I pulled my black hair back to tie it up in a purple ribbon.

"Not his fault?" she asked in disbelief. She was standing behind me, watching my reflection in the mirror, her hands placed dramatically at her hips. She had that you've-got-to-bekidding-me look on her face, as if she knew exactly what was going on—when, in reality, she had no idea.

To be honest, I thought my husband, Vic, was possessed. Sounds ridiculous, I know; but I'm certain that some vile entity was slowly eating away pieces of his soul in order to make room for its own. It was as if he was slowly losing parts of himself and gaining new ones; his artistic, romantic resolve had dissolved into a rich, ravaging rage.

"Not at all," I said. "Sure, he started the fight, but I'm the clumsy one."

She shook her head, frowning. "Lilly," she said stepping forward and placing a gentle hand on my shoulder. "You would tell me if there was more, right?"

I looked at her brown eyes in the mirror and offered a reassuring smile. "Of course I would. I tell you everything, you know that."

"What were you two fighting about, anyway?"

I chuckled, closed the medicine cabinet, and turned around to face her. "It was the stupidest thing. We were fighting over mushrooms."

"I hate mushrooms," Vic said, as if I had asked him to swallow glass. He vigorously scraped them off the chicken, off of the plate, and onto the mahogany table.

"No, you don't," I said, not paying much attention to him. I took a bite of the chicken.

"Don't tell me what the hell I like," he snapped. "I've always hated mushrooms." He took a large gulp of the Cabernet and slammed his fork against his plate, probably just to make a loud noise, emphasizing his distaste for my cooking.

"Mushrooms are in the chicken pesto lasagna that I make, which you said was your favorite." I didn't look at him. I was forking a mushroom.

"Well, it's not now," he said before finishing his wine.

"That's too bad. I was planning to make it for you tomorrow," I slowly raised my head until my gaze met his metallic grey eyes. I felt my lips curl upward on their own, smiling without thought.

He reached for the bottle and poured more wine into his glass. "Are you fucking with me right now?"

"Right now, no," I said, cutting off another piece of chicken.

He slammed his big fist down on the table hard enough to topple his wine glass. The stem snapped, and dark purple liquid spewed out onto the table. The bowl of his glass rolled off and burst on the floor.

"I didn't know Vic was such a dick," Juvia said as we left the bathroom. "He seemed like such a great guy. Rylie can't shut up about him sometimes."

Juvia's husband, Rylie, and Vic were partners in some international business venture. Rylie had developed some new technology for computers or something—I didn't quite understand it—and Vic, with his connections to funding and ruthless business prowess, had been the one to help take the company soaring.

Juvia followed me out of my bathroom and into the bedroom. We would continue with our normal routine of grabbing coffee before we drove over to the middle school.

I met Juvia a couple of years ago. We were both teachers, and we instantly became best friends. We'd grab happy hour together, gossip about our students' parents, or other teachers, and hit on men that we had no intention of bringing home with us … well, I guess that was actually more my thing than hers.

Today was field trip day, and we were taking our classes to a predator exhibit at the museum. The kids would learn all about how some animals use unusual and creative methods for catching their prey. I'd show them one of my favorites, a viper that used a worm-like tail as a lure. Smaller predators would chase after the tail, thinking they were about to fill their bellies, only to be devoured themselves.

"He isn't a dick all the time," I assured her. "I think he just needs to take some time off, you know? Maybe cancel his next business trip and just relax for a while. He's always so stressed."

Juvia gave me a slanted smile. She probably felt guilty. She was the reason Vic and I met in the first place; Juvia invited me to a benefit party, and Vic was there as well. She had been trying to get us to meet for over a month. She told me she thought we would be a good match, and that maybe I could help him move on from the unexpected loss of his fiancée.

My memory of our meeting was still so vivid: the party, the live French jazz music in the background, and the smell of basil from the hors d'oeurves the banquet servers carried around on wooden trays.

"There he is," Juvia said, motioning toward the man who easily must have been the most handsome person in the room. Dressed in a white and blue tux, which molded to every inch of his muscular body, he was shaking hands with a group of men, congratulating them on yet another successful year.

"Juvia," I said, playfully grabbing her arm, "You said he was attractive, but he's just downright edible." We chuckled. She examined my outfit one more time. I wore a tight-fitting red and black dress that was as classy as it was revealing. No sense sending the wrong signals; I was starving, and he was just the treat I needed.

"Isn't he, though? They don't make many like that," she said, her voice filled with lust.

"Hell, if I wasn't married to Ryley, I'd give him a taste, too."

"Ryley's a great guy," I said. "He's adorable, in that sexy-nerd type of way." She smiled playfully. "You are so sweet for doing this," I continued. "Even though I protested about the blind date thing."

"Hey, you need a man, he needs a woman, you are both gorgeous, and you can both make me some beautiful godchildren," she said, laughing. "It's a win-win for all of us."

I hugged her. A year before, she had confided in me that she found out she could never have her own kids. It was part of her motivation to become a teacher. I had told her then that since I didn't have any family left, she could be the godmother of my children.

"Give him hell," she said, brushing a strand of hair off my face and giving me a nudge forward.

"Oh, you have no idea," I said, advancing toward him like a tigress in red heels.

"Have you ever been to Greece?" That was the first question Vic ever asked me, after learning my name, of course. I loved the deep richness of his voice, the kind of voice that possessed a demanding strength.

"I've never had the luxury," I said. That was the first lie I ever told him. I had to look up at him; he must have stood around six feet five, if not a little taller. "But I heard that you and Rylie were just there on business."

"Mostly business," he said, with a grin. His metallic grey eyes scraped me up and down, the way I wanted his hands to touch me. "But the perks of the job are the traveling and sightseeing."

"And what sights did you see in Greece?" I asked. He peered into my eyes, such a vibrant shade of blue; in the right lighting, they appeared almost violet. Like a key to a locked gate, he stepped into the garden of my soul. From that moment on, I knew he would be mine.

At first, Vic worshipped me. He painted portraits on canvases of my beauty in bright gowns of his choosing. Quite the artist, with his exquisite use of lighting, color, texture, and detail. He made offerings to me of gold and diamond necklaces, emerald earrings, and eventually a personally designed ruby engagement ring. I added the jewelry to my growing collection. He gave me massages with his strong hands, caressed every curve and inch of my body, and catered to my every desire. He was mine.

He moved me into his home at three months. Proposed after six months. We married on our one-year anniversary, a small, elegant beach wedding with a few of my friends, and his family.

As my wedding gift, he presented me with a beautiful cello, an instrument I hadn't played in years. I was surprised he remembered that I told him I'd played as a youth. On our wedding night, he drew me in my red wedding gown, a color he loved on me, as I played him the only song I could recollect.

"The melody sounds so sad," he said, looking up from the paper, his handsome face revealing a hint of worry that perhaps I, too, might be sad. "Such a beautiful melody, but sad."

"It is a sad song," I replied solemnly over the low tone of the strings. "But it's the only song I remember. I never could read notes very well. I don't even remember what it's called."

"Do you remember who composed it?"

I stopped playing and we locked eyes for several moments. "Me."

A few weeks after the wedding, things started to change; weird things started to happen around the house. I was playing the cello—my song—alone in the bedroom, when I heard the crash of glass. Startled, I dropped the bow. I glanced over at Lamia's cage, half-expecting her to have broken free. As always, she was resting on the branch.

I looked behind me to find our wedding photo had fallen off the wall. Moving across the room to assess the damage, I discovered my smile in the picture was untouched. The glass had torn into Vic's face. I left the mess for someone else to clean up and returned to my song.

When Vic returned home that night, he found me in rare form. I was sitting in the bedroom, holding my old silver jewelry box to my chest, surrounded by the broken glass from the picture. The first thing he heard when he entered the room was my soft sobbing. I didn't tell him why I was crying; I think he assumed it had something to do with the photo. He placed gentle hands on my shoulders and kissed the top of my head.

"It's okay, Lilly pad," he whispered in my ear. "Are you hurt? Did the glass cut you?"

"No," I said.

I watched as he swept the glass off the hardwood floor, still clutching the box to my chest. He missed a piece. I saw it by the bed and said nothing. As a result, he stepped on the glass barefoot as he crawled into bed with me. He cursed under his breath. I was immediately there to help. I pulled the glass out and blood flowed freely, so much blood for such a small cut.

"It's not too bad, sweetheart," I said, dabbing at his foot. He sat on the edge of the bed, watching me as I worked.

"Eh, I'll do a formal sweep of the room tomorrow," he said. "Glad it was me who stepped on it and not you."

Looking up at him, he beamed at me, despite his injury. I smiled back. He truly was beautiful man.

"You might be limping for the next two days," I said, placing a large pink Band Aid on the cut.

He chuckled at the color. "You take such good care of me." He lifted my chin so I could meet his eyes. "You are going to make a wonderful mother one day."

My smile stretched all the way across my face and reached my ears. I stood up and he pulled me onto his lap.

"You seem cheerier now," he said.

"That's because you are home." I slid my fingers through his dark hair. "You have been gone so much lately."

"I know, and I'm sorry," he said with guilt in his voice. "We should probably just cancel my next business trip then, shouldn't we?" He held me tight and kissed my neck. "And I don't know, run away to Europe, maybe?"

"We can't just …"

"Ryley can handle one trip on his own."

"I have work, too; I have my students," I said. He kissed me. "But … cough, cough … I think I might be getting the flu. A really bad flu."

"Yeah, you should probably take the rest of the week off." We smiled, chuckled, and kissed. "God, I love you."

"Where should we go?" I asked, our foreheads pressed against each other.

"Greece," he said. "I'll start packing." I stood up from his lap and picked up the bloody glass piece and red-soaked towel, and took them to the bathroom. I locked the door.

The trip was just what we needed. A romantic getaway of dancing, wine, fine dining, and visiting sites of myth. We stayed in the most luxurious suites at each hotel, visited an art gallery, and I purchased statues of Lamia and Hecate for our bedroom at home. Vic wasn't a fan of them, but I didn't care. He didn't seem to understand their significance.

When we returned to the real world, after our extravagant European escape, I experienced another oddity. I awoke in the middle of the night, wet from sweat. I had a dream that I knew terrified me, yet I couldn't remember what the dream was about.

I remembered fire and circling shadows, but this wasn't overly strange to me. I often dreamed of hell, and what it would be like to go there. I glanced over at a sleeping Vic and could hear his low snore. But that wasn't the only sound I heard. At first, I thought someone might be shoveling snow outside in the middle of the night. But as my dreamy brain cleared, I realized it was mid-spring, not snow season. The scraping sound was coming from our bedroom, directly below us, under the bed. I instantly sat up, my entire body flushed with new heat. Something was slowly scratching, clawing, at the hardwood floor.

I almost called Vic's name, but I stopped myself. The noise stopped. I think it knew that I was awake. I listened to the silence for an entire minute before I slid over to the edge of the bed and looked down at the floor. I knew I didn't imagine it. Something was there.

I could feel its presence slithering under me, its heat in the air. The faintest smell of something burning. Cautiously, I pulled up the bed skirt and slowly lowered my head to search the darkness below. Despite the heat, I was chilled to my core. Whatever it was, it had the greenest eyes I'd ever seen.

I didn't tell Vic about what I saw. He would probably think I was crazy, or at just dreaming. I knew I wasn't dreaming. I didn't sleep for the rest of that night. I lay there, listening for it to resume sharpening its claws, but it didn't stir. It didn't make a sound. Eventually the room cooled, and I knew it had left.

Vic wouldn't have believed me, even if I told him. He didn't believe in the supernatural, or even the spiritual, for that matter. I knew that the demonic entity was real. I could feel an echo of its presence, a type of heat, hatred, and rage. It seemed to encompass the air in the house.

Although Vic didn't know that this entity existed, he was still affected by the influence of its hellish echo. He became easily irritable, and aggressive.

I had never seen him express his temper in any way, yet I always knew he had one—if that makes sense. He started to freak out over little things. He wasn't able to find his favorite tie, so he threw all of his clothes—and mine—across the room and onto the floor. A few days later, he crushed his cell phone in fury because I didn't answer his ten back-to-back missed calls, apparently forgetting that I had parent-teacher conferences that night.

A week later, Vic and I had our first fight. I came home from happy hour with Juvia, and he accused me of sleeping around. It was completely unwarranted, and the accusation came out of nowhere. He was sitting on the couch, in the dark, aside from the pale light of the setting sun oozing in from the window drapes. The situation reminded me of a parent, waiting for their rebellious teenager to come home after curfew.

"I was out drinking," I said calmly. I collapsed on the red satin rocking chair across from him. "Have you been drinking?"

"Not a sip," he hissed. He might have been lying, but the look on his face prevented me from prying farther. He looked so angry, so hurt, and so very, very desperate. It wasn't a look I had ever seen on his face. I didn't like it. I didn't like for him to look so weak.

"Maybe you should have one. It looks like you could use a buzz."

This angered him. That was a look I was more comfortable with; yet anger has a price, too. He accused me of never being there for him, despite the fact that he was the one who was always gone. He traveled a lot, and I guess that meant that I was supposed to make sure to be home to pamper him when he wasn't on a work trip. To him, it might have sounded reasonable. But I wasn't a girl to ask for permission. I just did things, and I dealt with the consequences as they came.

Still, being angry with me for not making time for him was one thing; accusing me of sucking another guy's dick, however, was a bit much. Especially when he was such a perfect specimen in every way. I didn't need another body to please me. His was all I could ever hope for.

A week later, things escalated into our first physical confrontation. I was looking through the canvases Vic had painted of me. The ones he didn't hang up around the house, he kept stacked upright in boxes in his closet, specifically the ones that captured the true radiance of my body. Painting my body never got old for him, and posing never got old for me. I spotted my favorite: me naked in a chair in front of the fire, and Lamia draped over my shoulders. From the lighting of the flames, to the curves of my body, I admired Vic's attention to detail.

I placed the canvas back in the box and opened another. That's when I found them. In an instant, all flattery fled, and rage ripped through me as I yanked the box from the closet and hurled it across the floor, while paintings of his last duchess spilled out across the room. He had accused me of cheating, and here he was, still carrying around his baggage of dead-hooker weight in our closet.

I waited for him to return home. I wanted him there to watch as I lit the fireplace, to see that dead bitch burn in front of him. The canvases lit up instantly. He didn't need her. He had me. He was mine. I had never seen a man so angry. A sudden shift in his brain from joyful to screaming, thrashing rage. Anger that completely dissolved all that he was, and he regressed into a carnal beast. The loud sounds that escaped his jaws were almost inhuman. He ran for the fire, as if he was going to grab the burning canvases with his bare hands. Reason overcame his rage, as his hands felt the searing heat.

"You bitch," he growled softly, nastily.

I stood over him, watching his pathetic display, him on his knees by the fire, like a child whose favorite toy was just destroyed. My skin burned from the heat of my blood as I saw his tears.

"She's dead!" I screamed. "She can't have you!"

He stood up, and a second later, my head hit the ground, his body on top of mine, his hands grasping my throat. His face was red, veins burst from his neck and the sides of his head. His eyes, his eyes, his silver eyes cut me. He squeezed harder. For less than a second, his eyes flashed green.

Despite the lack of oxygen, I didn't struggle. I gently touched his face. I closed my eyes, and I found myself drifting off into darkness. His dead lover's face flashed before me, her dark skin, even darker eyes, her brown wavy hair. I knew this side of him existed, yet I had never seen it, never felt it. I opened the gates to my garden, those eyes that I knew were always violet in the firelight, and met his gaze. He stared into me, all strength leaving him, and he collapsed on top of me. I gently ran my fingers through his hair, listening to our heavy breathing. It was over. The bitch was gone, and he was mine once again.

The next morning Vic woke me with a mimosa. We had slept on the couch, warmed by the fire. I didn't even notice he had gotten up, cooked breakfast, opened champagne. He knelt down on the floor beside the couch, and kissed my tender neck and lips.

"Words can't express how sorry I am," he said weakly. I hated the way his voice changed; it was softer, higher, and I hated the look of helplessness on his face. This was not the man I married.

"Vic, it's no one's fault but mine," I said, touching his face. I was no stranger to loss, and I understood his pain more than anyone, how difficult it can be moving on.

"No, I …"

"Shhhh," I said. "Stop talking." I sipped the champagne, and then offered him a drink. "Vic, I want a baby."

"You're ready?" he asked. His defeated tone rose to the level of excitement. I nodded, "I've been ready a very long time."

I chuckled as the two girls buried their faces in my chest, cowering away from the bizarre-looking snake. I realized I had found a new favorite, a snake that was discovered not many years ago. The spider-tailed viper, native to Iran. The snake laid camouflaged against the rocks, and wriggled its tail to attract prey; the ball with little tentacles looked just like a crawling spider, and made for a wonderful lure for birds.

"It can't get you from behind the glass," I said to the girls. The boys were clearly enjoying this exhibit much more than most of the girls. I turned and saw Juvia standing with a group of kids in front of another cage, one containing a turtle, I think.

"It just looks so creepy," one of the girls said, pulling away.

"All right, we can move along," I said. "It's nice to get out of the classroom, isn't it?" I called over to Juvia.

"Yeah, except next time, I get to pick the field trip," she joked and forced a smile. She couldn't stop examining my face.

"One of my students, Taylor, told me I look very pretty today," I said as we walked along the exhibit. The placard at the reptile display said the zookeepers were going to do a feeding demonstration soon.

"You always look pretty," she said. I thought I detected a hint of jealousy, which wasn't an uncommon thing.

"I'm still worried about you," she said quietly after the girls at my side followed the tour group. "Maybe you two should take a break."

"From my husband? No, it's nothing we can't work through."

"Promise me you will tell me if anything like this happens again."

"Of course I will."

I made a point to avoid returning home until late that night. I had drinks with Juvia after work at a wine bar that had half-priced bottles every Wednesday. Not that price ever mattered, not with our husband's bank accounts. I think our low teacher salaries kept us humbler than most rich women.

"Are you sure you don't want to stay over at my house tonight?" she asked. Her constant harping was starting to annoy me.

"No, no," I said. "I promise you everything is fine. Besides, we never know when our boys are leaving next, or where they might be going. I find myself missing him all the time."

"I think Argentina is next on the list," she said bitterly. "Spain, that's where the four of us need to go this summer."

"You have a deal," I said. "Another getaway, that's exactly what we need."

After drinks, instead of returning home, I went

shopping for more makeup and then stopped for sushi. Vic called me five times, but I didn't answer.

As it grew dark, I drove to the woods to watch the moon. I took my cello out of the trunk, and began walking into the trees. I didn't need a flashlight, the super moon was bright enough to light my path.

After a half mile or so, I found a rock to sit atop, and I played my song for the moon goddess Hecate, a lullaby to the owls, and the little mammals in the trees, and the snakes at my feet slithered to the vibrations of the strings.

Vic was already asleep by the time I returned. He left the kitchen light on, and a caramel and chocolate covered apple on the counter. That was his way of apologizing. He knew it was my favorite dessert. Such a sweetheart. I took a bite, savoring the sweet taste of the caramel, swirling with the sourness of the green apple. The kitchen lights flickered, and I looked up at the ceiling. It wasn't just the kitchen lights.

My eyes traveled down the hall, and I realized all of the lights were flickering. A sudden shiver rocked my body.

The kitchen light went out with a fizzing noise. I dropped the apple on the floor, and I made my way to the stairs in the dark and flicked on the hallway light. Within a few seconds, that light started to fade in and out as well.

I knew it was up there. Vic would have no idea. I ran up the stairs and burst into the bedroom. I froze when I saw its tall and slender silhouette, standing on the bed, looking down at Vic as he slept. It was reaching out its long skinny claws toward his face. Immediately, its head turned to me, its bright green eyes locked onto my body. Its stare tore into me, and struck my soul. I felt exposed, as if it knew me, all of me. It turned back to Vic and howled in rage. Somehow Vic didn't stir, but the hallway light behind me exploded, sending glass shards raining to the carpet, and darkness swallowed me. I didn't scream; I don't think I could have if I wanted to. In silence, I turned to leave, but the door slammed in front of me.

"Lilly," I heard Vic's voice in my ear. I spun around to find him standing right behind me in the dark.

Somehow, in an instant, he had moved out of the bed and across the room. His strong hands grasped my arms, and my back was forced against the wall. His bare chest pressed against me. His mouth found my neck. His teeth touched my skin. My nails scraped up his back, and I wrapped my arms around his neck. He grasped my thighs, lifted me, and slammed me on the bed, his body pressing against mine. His hands went up, his head went down, and I was consumed by darkness.

Even in my dreams that night, he was ravishing me; we fucked on a bed of fire as his body burned away. My body remained flawless, despite the flames.

I could tell Lamia was hungry again. Her appetite was insatiable as of late, highly unusual for a snake who only eats once every two weeks. I watched her, snaking her way back and forth on the branch; it looked like she was pacing. I reached my hand into the cage and placed it on the end of the branch. She stopped moving. Her pink tongue flicked in and out of her red lips. She coiled her head around my wrist and slowly slithered up my arm, her cool scales caressing my soft skin.

The rodents weren't enough to fill her. I knew I'd have to feed her some much larger prey soon. Maybe a rabbit this time.

When I told Vic I was pregnant, I had never seen him so happy, aside from when I told him I would marry him. He picked me up in his strong arms and twirled me around the room.

"I promise you, everything is going to change," he said to me. "I'm going to change. I promise you, things are going to get better."

I believed him. Things were going to get better, and our daughter was going to have the best life this world had to offer.

"It's going to be a girl," I said seriously.

"And how would you know that already?"

"Just a hunch. My eggs only accept the female sperm," I said with a smirk.

He laughed, "Well, what if I want a boy?"

"You would make a great dad to either," I kissed him, and gently bit his neck.

"Let's celebrate," he said, kissing me. "Tonight, after work."

"It's a date. Now, run me a hot bath."

"Yes, ma'am," he said, kissing me one more time. He walked over to the bathroom to fulfill my request.

He didn't even notice that Lamia wasn't in her cage.

Every detail of tonight needed to be perfect: the food, the lighting, the smells, the atmosphere. I filled the entire house with candles, lit the sconces on the walls, lit candles on the tables and shelves, and burned incense of cherry and hibiscus. I made a rack of braised lamb with asparagus and potatoes. Low cello music slithered from the speakers, and I wore the same red and black dress I had on when we first met.

"How did I ever get so lucky to marry a woman like you?" he asked when he entered the house.

"Luck has little to do with it, darling," I said, undoing his tie for him. "You deserve to have me." I removed his tie and undid his buttons. "You earned me."

He pulled me into him. "Well, whatever I did to deserve you, I'm sure glad I did it."

We kissed our way to the couch and collapsed in a tangle of limbs. "I just want to be yours forever," he whispered in my ear.

"You will be," I said, nibbling on his neck. "I'm so happy to have you. You are perfect."

I sat up and he rested his head in my lap, listening to the music. I placed my hand on his chest, feeling it rise and fall. I looked down at him in my lap.

"Until the sun collapses, you will be mine."

He smiled up at me. "I've been thinking of baby names all day," he said blissfully. "Mostly for girls." He shook his head, still obviously doubting that I knew the sex of the baby.

"I've chosen a name already," I said. "Lilith, after her mother."

"You don't think that should be something we decide together?" he asked, a hint of irritation in his voice.

I cackled. "No, Vic, it's not. You don't really get a say."

His smile disappeared. "Lilly, what the hell has gotten into you? It's our baby; it's not just your decision."

"It's not your baby."

It didn't take long for that look to appear on his face. The rage. But the rage didn't stay for long. His eyes saw into mine, they were undoubtedly violet and aglow, and this time I didn't show him the garden of Eden, I showed him the hell from my dreams. He saw flames. He saw tortured souls screaming in anguish. He saw the devil himself and all his servants.

Instead of growling, he whimpered. His breathing turned heavy, fast; he was struggling to fill his lungs with air. He tried to avert his gaze, but he couldn't. He was burning away in the hellfire of my eyes. His body wriggled, struggled beneath the heat of my gaze. I could feel his heart pounding, his chest rising and falling, rising and falling, rising and falling, until it rose no longer. I swallowed his soul whole.

His empty body lay still. I stood up and rested his dead head on the pillow. I could feel Vic inside me, wriggling around in the hell in my belly. He would be with me forever, as we both had wished.

I went to the kitchen to warm the lamb in the oven. Then I went upstairs to my closet. I pulled off the red wedding ring and added it to my collection. I sifted through the jewels until I found an old silver ring, with a serpent carved into it, a green emerald in its eye.

I slid it onto my ring finger. I went into the bathroom and removed my dress. I stood naked in the mirror and turned to the side. I hadn't begun to show, but I knew the baby was there. I could feel her slithering around inside my womb, as the serpent Lamia, now imprinted on my flesh, slithered around my body.

I didn't bother replacing my clothes before I returned downstairs to eat. Vic had satisfied my unearthly appetite, but my body still needed a good meal. I froze in the kitchen doorway, my skin suddenly hot. Vic's body had moved from the couch to the mahogany table. He, too, was naked, and he was eating the lamb with his hands.

A plate had been set for me, across from him. He looked up at me with those green eyes and smiled a toothy grin. I placed a hand on my belly, and I smiled back.

THE DOLLHOUSE TREE

The tree was hollow and gray and leafless. It was the only lifeless tree out of hundreds that resided on the property, yet it towered over the others. The children climbed it excitedly, hanging from the twisted branches, singing songs and laughing loudly. The dead leaves crunched beneath their feet as they jumped down and danced around the skeletal oak, only to climb back up the tree again.

The wind picked up, dragging leaves across the ground before hurling them in vortices around the children. The sky was darkening, and the clouds were getting heavy.

"Russell, where did those children come from?" Lucile asked, while staring out the window.

She ran her fingers across the soft fabric of the rusty

red curtains. She'd been watching them for several minutes, making sure they didn't pick any squash or pumpkins from her garden.

"What children?" he called loudly from his office.

He poked his bald head around the corner, not bothering to get up from his chair. The candlelight behind him cast a shadow across the left side of his face. At the moment, he was working on his latest novel. His previous one had been published two years before, and his first novel, a few years before that. He chose to flee the busy city in favor of creative and stimulating solitude, and moved the family into a manor on the outskirts of Vermillion, Ohio. Russell chose the place because of its size, and impossibly low price. Mr. Talbot had been trying to sell the old manor for years, and was desperate for money.

"There are children outside our house, and I don't see any adults with them. They shouldn't be playing all the way out here without supervision, especially those girls. They shouldn't be roughhousing with boys; it's unladylike."

"Well, you're watching them, aren't you?" he joked. "That's supervision."

Lucile was silent for a while, unable to move from the window. One of the girls took off her bonnet and swung it around by its strings. One of the boy's suspender straps hung down at his sides, and they whipped around as he spun. There were holes on the knees of his pants. They all cheered loudly as one of the girls reached the top of the tree.

Such peculiar children, Lucile thought.

"Russell, they are playing around that dead tree. Come look! That tree is old and brittle. The way they are hanging from those weak branches, they could fall and break their necks, and their parents would probably hold us responsible."

"Lucile, will you stop worrying so much?" Russell asked tiredly, not even bothering to poke his head around the corner this time. "I'm sure I remember Mr. Talbot mentioning something about children who live around here. Where is Bethany? She should be outside with them. She needs to make some new friends."

"She is upstairs in her room. I don't think she should be playing with those children; look at them. They are wearing such old, tattered, and dirty clothing. They look like orphans." She noticed that one boy was holding a thin black rope.

"Orphans or no orphans, our daughter needs friends," he said sternly.

She turned from the window to look back at his office, hoping he could see her distasteful look.

"She hates it here," he continued, his head still down. He dipped his pen in ink and continued to scribble. "And that's exactly what I was afraid of when we decided to move. Call for her. Send her out to play."

"She's tired," Lucile argued, "and it's about to rain. She can go make friends tomorrow."

She turned back to the window and gasped. Her face grew hot from embarrassment.

All of the children had paused in their playing, and were staring at her through the window. She also noticed that the black rope the boy was holding wasn't actually a rope at all. It was moving, wriggling around his arms.

It was a snake.

She quickly closed the curtains as if that would make the children disappear. "I'm going to finish supper," she called, breathing heavily as she made her way toward the kitchen. "The potatoes should be soft by now."

As her face cooled, she suddenly felt cold on her back, and her knees were quivering as she walked. She didn't like the way the children were looking at her.

Lucile shot up from her bed, heart pounding, her entire body wet from sweat. She felt as if she had just awakened from a nightmare, yet she couldn't recall her dream at all. She glanced over at Russell, still asleep. As deep a sleeper as he was, the house could burn down around him, and he would never know.

She lay back down on the bed, resting her head on the soft pillow. She closed her eyes and as she drifted back into sleep, she could make out the faintest sound of a child's excited giggle.

"Bethany," Lucile called the next morning as she gently knocked on the door of her daughter's bedroom. "Bethany, I'm coming in."

She opened the door just a crack; it creaked loudly from the rusted bolts. She could already see the girl's bed was empty. The white sheets were hanging off the side and touching the floor. She pushed the door open the rest of the way and entered.

"Bethany, are you in here?"

There was no answer.

"That girl …" She hurried to the bed to tidy it up. "She should know better than to leave a messy room."

She returned downstairs.

"Bethany!" she called louder. "Russell, have you seen our daughter?"

Russell poked his head around the corner of his office.

"The kids came by earlier this morning. She went outside to play."

Lucile eyed him with contempt and hurried to the window.

"You let her play with those orphans? Did you get her dressed and bathed?" She asked him this as if he were a forgetful child.

"She is dressed appropriately, and she can bathe when she gets back inside. She's going to get dirty and sweaty playing outside anyway."

"What about breakfast?" She pulled back the curtain, searching for the children. Her eyes immediately went to the dead oak tree.

"For goodness' sake, she ate an apple. In fact, I gave all the children apples."

What she saw at the tree flooded her heart with fear.

"BETHANY!" she screamed in horror.

She rushed for the door, almost losing her footing on the smooth wooden floor. She burst outside, screaming her daughter's name again.

"Bethany!"

She sprinted across the grass, lifting the floor-length skirt of her wide dress.

"Bethany!"

She stopped at the base of the tree and looked up. Bethany wasn't up there. She held her hand to her chest, feeling the rumbling of her heart. How was that possible? From the window, she had seen her daughter at the top of the tree, dangling down, about to fall. She looked around at the surrounding trees. There were no children in sight.

"We are glad you moved here, Bethany," a pretty blonde girl said.

She was the oldest of the children, at fourteen years of age, four years older than Bethany.

"I'm Angela."

Angela was the only one in the group who appeared well-kept. Her long hair was styled in spiraling curls, and the white dress she wore was stain-free, despite playing outside.

"It's nice to meet you, Angela."

They skipped arm in arm through the trees, and the other children followed. They all carried with them sincere smiles, except for one; Daemon was his name. He was around twelve years old, with dirty matted hair, icy eyes, and a closed-off, harsh expression on his face. Bethany was a little afraid of him. He hadn't said a word since she met him.

"Where are we going?" she asked.

Bethany hadn't spent much time exploring the land around her parents' property. Her mother hardly allowed her to leave the house, instead insisting that she learn what it means to be a proper lady. The children were happy and eager to show her the woods, something she'd been afraid to do on her own. She would surely get lost if she were alone. Even now with the children, if they'd left her, she didn't think she would be able to find her way back.

"We are going to the doll maker," said Mary, the youngest at six years of age. She skipped on ahead of them. "He makes the most beautiful dolls."

She was Angela's little sister, just as blonde and pretty, even though she was covered in dirt and grime. Bethany knew her mother would never approve of her coming home covered in filth. She hoped she didn't get her dress too dirty, or her mother would forbid her to play with the other children again.

"A doll maker?"

"Oh yes," Angela said. "He loves children, and he will make a doll in your likeness."

"I didn't bring any coins with me."

"You don't need money, sweet girl," she said. "He does it for all of the children who come to see him."

She said it as if it were the most obvious thing in the world. The children came to a broken-down building, with vines growing up the walls. Half of the building was charred from fire; the other half was covered in soot and ash.

"This is where he lives," Angela said.

"It doesn't look like anyone could live here," Bethany said. "It doesn't look safe to go inside."

"He lives in the basement," Mary cried excitedly. She was jumping up and down, her hair waving in the breeze. "It was spared from the fire. He still makes dolls."

"Was this his house?" Bethany asked.

She didn't make a move toward the building. She didn't want to go inside.

"It was a place for children with nowhere to go," Angela said softly.

Her smile faded away and she closed her eyes, as if to hold back a tear.

"It still is," Daemon said dryly.

It was the first time he'd spoken. The other children looked to him, smiling and nodding on his behalf. He moved forward and grabbed Bethany's hand. He squeezed it reassuringly. That's when Bethany noticed the snake. A black snake was coiled around his other arm, its head resting in his free hand. She almost cried out, but she bit her tongue instead. She didn't want to look like a coward in front of her new friends.

"Come on," he said. "He'd love to meet you."

"I can't find her anywhere," Lucile cried in a panic. "How could you just let her wander off?"

"She's with all those kids. There's lots of woods to explore. She'll be back."

Russel didn't bother looking up from his desk.

"You never let her play outside. That's what a kid needs. Let your daughter have some fun."

"She can have fun all she wants," Lucile snapped. "She just needs to stay close to home. If something happens to her, I'm holding you responsible."

He still didn't look up, didn't even respond as he continued working, crossing out something he'd written and grabbing a fresh piece of parchment.

"You can be so hysterical sometimes," he muttered under his breath.

She let loose a high-pitched groan and left him alone in his office. *How could he be so careless,* she wondered. Those orphans were no good. Bethany should be associating with children of her own caliber. Now they were off somewhere doing heaven knows what. She stopped by the window again and looked out. She let out another bloodcurdling scream. Lucile ran outside once again, certain that what she saw was real this time.

"Bethany!" she screamed angrily as she sprinted across the grass.

"Yes, Mama?" the little girl called from the tree.

She sat atop one of the branches beside a young boy around the age of twelve. His brown hair was dirty and matted; his once-white shirt was now a light brown, and his pants were torn at the knee. He wore no shoes.

"Get down from that tree right now," Lucile demanded. "What's gotten into you? This is dangerous."

That's when she noticed that her daughter was holding a slender black snake in her hands.

"What …"

"Hello, Mrs. Holland," a blonde girl called sweetly.

The only proper-looking child in the bunch, her hair was done in curls, and her dress was a sparkling white. She appeared to be the oldest. She sat at the base of the tree beside a younger version of herself. They both shared the same facial features and green eyes. Lucile halted her hysterics at the sound of her name. She gave each child a once-over. There were six of them, not counting Bethany, three girls and three boys.

"I'm sorry, Mommy!" Bethany called, making no move to get down from the tree. She glanced over at the boy beside her. "It just seemed like fun."

Lucile noticed the snake was coiled several times around her wrist.

"Please just come down," Lucile pleaded, trying to calm herself, her eyes moving from the snake to the boy.

Something about the boy made Lucile's body shudder suddenly, as if the temperature around her had dropped to zero. He was the only one of the children who wasn't smiling. Instead, he was almost glaring at the woman.

"Don't mind Daemon," said the blonde girl as she stood up. "He's all bark and no bite." She brushed off the bottom of her dress. "I'm Angela."

"It's nice to meet you." Lucile forced the words out. "All of you."

Her tone wasn't at all sincere.

"It's okay, Bethany," said Angela. "Come down."

Lucile was surprised that Bethany obeyed this girl instead of her own mother. Bethany unraveled the snake from her wrist and handed it to the boy. Then she slowly and carefully scooted away from the boy and toward the trunk. It took her an agonizingly long minute to safely reach the grass below. Lucile rushed to her daughter and hugged her.

"Don't ever climb this tree again! And don't ever let me catch you playing with snakes!"

"Yes, Mommy," Bethany muttered, disappointed.

"Now come inside." Lucile took the girl's hand and dragged her away from the children and the dead tree.

"See you later, Bethany!" the children all called together in unison. They waved, and Bethany waved back, sadly.

"Lucile, you have got to stop sheltering Bethany," Russell said. He sat at the kitchen table, sipping tea. "She needs to be free to be a child."

"She was climbing that tree," Lucile said, looking out

the window. The kids were still outside, playing a game where each kid had to jump over the other. "What was I supposed to do? Let her kill herself?"

"You don't know that she would have been hurt," he said. "I'm not saying I like her playing in the tree, but she needs to be free to make some of her own choices."

"She is a child!"

"A very bright child. Lucile, you make every decision for her—what she wears, how her hair is supposed to look, what she does all day long, what she eats, what she plays with." He paused to take another sip of tea. "If you make every decision for her, you are leaving our daughter with only one choice." He locked eyes with his wife. "To disobey you. It's only a matter of time."

"I want that tree cut down," Lucile said sternly, ignoring his words. "Tomorrow!"

Russell sighed and stood up. He returned to his office without a word.

Lucile awoke in another cold sweat. This time she was breathing heavily. Again, she couldn't remember her dream, but vaguely recalled pale, icy eyes. She sat up, listening to Russell's low snores. Her leg was asleep. She climbed out of bed and stretched, forcing blood to flow down to her toes. She found herself moving toward the window, not really understanding why. She stood there, staring out at the dead tree. The gray bark seemed to sparkle in the moonlight. It was oddly beautiful.

"Daddy, please don't," Bethany cried, as she followed her father from the backyard and around the side of the house. He carried an axe in his hands.

"I'm sorry, lovebug, but I have to. You know how your mother is."

"I hate her!" she muttered softly.

"Now, now, Bethany, you don't hate your mother." He glanced back at the girl. "You're just upset."

She was silent. She glanced around the yard for the children. They were nowhere to be found. She crossed her arms over her chest and glared at her mother, who stood inside the house, at her bedroom window.

After three good swings, Russell broke a hole in the dead, hollow trunk. He was surprised he did it so easily, even more surprised that the branches had held under the children's weight. He hacked at the tree a few more times before Bethany cried out.

"What's the matter?" he asked, turning around and setting the axe against the tree.

"Look," she pointed into the hole. "There's something inside the tree."

Russell bent over to get a better look, and sure enough, he saw something. He reached his arm into the tree and grasped the object. It was firm and smooth, cold to the touch.

"It's a doll," he said, pulling the thing out of the tree. "A porcelain doll."

"Let me see," Bethany said, quickly taking the toy from him. She examined it, raking her fingers through the doll's blonde hair.

"How did that get in there?" he asked.

"There's a hole at the top," Bethany answered. She sounded far away, deep in her own thoughts.

She carried the doll away from the tree and moved toward the house. Russell watched her as she moved across the yard. That's when he saw them, the children. They sat cross-legged on the grass in front of his porch, in a straight line. They all watched him expectantly. He wondered how he'd missed them. They didn't seem at all alarmed or upset that he was cutting down their tree.

Bethany, however, hung her head low, ashamed. She waved to them as she walked up the porch steps and hurried into the house. *This is going to be awkward,* he thought. He glanced up at the house and saw his wife, staring at him through the window. He shook his head at her and raised the axe. He hacked at the tree once again, but wood only collided with wood. Suddenly feeling the lightness of the handle, he stared down in wide-eyed surprise at the axe head, resting in the grass.

"Well, I guess that's that," he said, picking it up. He carried the broken ax back around the house to the shed.

"What do you mean, the axe broke?" Lucile demanded.

"It happens sometimes." Russell shrugged. He crossed his legs and leaned back in the wooden rocking chair.

"Get a new one!"

"Settle down, Lucile," Russell said, exasperated. "Bethany has agreed not to climb up the tree anymore, so what's the problem?"

Lucile started to say something, but stopped.

Russell knew what she wanted to say, why she really wanted the tree cut down. She wanted the children to go away. Russell agreed that the children were a bit creepy, especially the way they had all watched him today.

"Bethany, why do those children play around here?" Lucile asked. "Have they told you where they come from?"

Bethany sat on the red velvet-cushioned couch, playing with the doll. She didn't seem to hear her mother at all.

"Bethany!" Lucile called loudly.

She reached for the doll, attempting to snatch it from the girl's hands. Bethany didn't let go.

"Give it to me," Lucile demanded, tugging harder.

Bethany didn't respond and didn't look up—she just held on to the doll.

"Lucile, calm down," Russell said.

Lucile ignored him and tugged harder, too hard. Bethany cried out as the doll was ripped from her hands and fell onto the wooden floor with a crack.

"Look what you did!" Bethany cried, horrified.

"Look what I did! I just wanted to see the doll and you wouldn't let go."

Lucile knelt down and picked it up. The face was cracked, and one of the eyes had caved in.

"You broke it!" Bethany screamed. She snatched the doll from her mother's hands and ran out of the room.

Lucile sighed, "What's gotten into that girl?"

"I think the children have been coming here for awhile, Lucile," Russell said, getting up from his chair. "Since before we moved here. I honestly think Mr. Talbot was letting some of the kids stay here."

Lucile didn't say anything; instead she just stood there and watched as he followed Bethany out of the room.

"Bethany." a child's voice called, barely a whisper. "Wake up, Bethany."

The little girl rolled over on her side, not quite awake.

"Come along, Bethany," the voice whispered invitingly. "Come play with me."

Bethany could hear the voice in her dream, but she didn't wake up.

"Bethany!" the voice called loudly, no longer a whisper, no longer childlike. It was deep, distorted. She awoke in a fright, nearly jumping up and out of the bed.

"Who's there?" she called into the darkness.

There was no answer, no sound at all besides the wind howling outside.

"Hello," she called again.

She heard something drop onto the floor, and she jumped up, standing on her bed, her pillow clutched in her hands. She peered into the darkness, searching for the source of the noise. She could barely make out the shelf on her wall, where several of her stuffed toys and dolls sat. There was a space missing. The broken doll had been sitting there. She heard a tinny pitter-patter of something scurrying across the floor, and she gasped. She saw the tiny silhouette of something moving, and in a blur, it was gone. It had run under her bed.

"Bethany," she heard a voice call from below her.

Her hands were quivering. She wanted to scream, but she couldn't find her voice.

"Come and play, Bethany …" the voice said.

She thought the voice sounded familiar. She inched toward the edge of the bed and looked down at the empty floor. There was more rustling beneath her.

"Come out," she called, her voice barely a whisper.

There was no answer. The girl summed up the courage and leapt off the bed, ready to run for the door, but immediately something grasped her ankle. She fell, the pillow breaking her fall, and screamed as something dragged her under the bed and into total darkness.

"It's me, silly," Daemon called.

He lay beside her under the bed.

"You are such a chicken." He laughed proudly. "I scared you."

"Yes, you scared me to death," she snapped angrily. "How did you even get in here?"

And what about the doll, she wondered.

"Never mind that," he said. "Come on, we have something for you." He slithered out from under the bed, and reached out his hand to help her.

Her fear quickly vanished, and she took his hand excitedly. When she stood up, she looked outside the window. She could see Angela standing by the tree, looking up at her. She was glowing, in her beautiful white dress. Her little sister Mary stood beside her. Angela whispered something into her younger sister's ear, and Mary took off in a sprint toward the house.

"Come on," Daemon called, gently pulling.

He smiled at her. She didn't resist. She followed him out of the room.

For the third night in a row, Lucile awoke in the middle of the night, and this time she was sure she heard a child laughing.

"Bethany?" she called.

Russell didn't stir; he remained asleep. She heard the giggling again, coming from right outside her bedroom door.

"I'm here, Mommy," she heard Bethany say.

Then she heard footsteps quickly moving across the floor and down the stairs. Lucile got up out of bed and hurried out of the room.

"What are you doing awake?" she asked when she entered the hallway. "It's time to go back to bed."

She heard her daughter's soft laughter from the living room downstairs.

"Come get me, Mommy."

"I have something for you," Angela said when Bethany and Daemon reached her at the bottom of the tree. "Something special."

She handed Bethany a doll, similar to the one Bethany had found earlier. Only this one was different, it had brown hair—like her own—and dark eyes. It looked just like her.

"Thank you," Bethany said sweetly. She hugged the doll. "I love it. Thank Mr. Talbot for me, please."

"You can thank him yourself," she said. "But first, you must do something, something brave."

"First, you just have to put it in the hole," Daemon said, placing a hand on her shoulder. "The hole at the top of the tree."

"But I like my doll," she said sadly. "I don't want to lose her."

"You can play with the doll whenever you want," Angela said. "In fact, after you do this, the doll will play back."

"Play back?" Bethany took a step away from the children. "What do you mean?"

"You'll see," the older girl said. "It's so much fun. Just climb up. Don't you trust us?"

"I'm not supposed to climb the tree," Bethany said.

"Why not? Because your mother said so?" Daemon taunted. "You want to be one of us, don't you?"

"It's your choice," Angela said, her tone soft and quiet. She was nodding her head, pleased, as if she knew she would make the right choice.

"One of us! One of us!" the other children called.

They were sitting atop different branches of the tree. Bethany could have sworn that they weren't there a moment ago.

"What about this hole?" she asked, moving toward the one that Russell had made in the bark. But the hole was gone. "How did …"

"It's a special tree," Angela said, smiling. "Soon, you will be able to taste its fruit. The sweetest there ever was."

"Now climb," Daemon demanded. "Unless you want to be told what to do all your life."

"No way!" Bethany cried.

She clutched the doll to her chest with one arm, and used the other to grab the lowest branch. She used her feet to push up off the trunk, and she began to climb.

"Bethany, I'm tired of playing these games with you!" Lucile said sternly. "Stop hiding from me! It's time for bed."

"I'm over here, Mommy," the little girl said.

Lucile thought it came from the kitchen. She took a step toward the door when she heard the voice behind her call out:

"Not there, over here."

Lucile groaned; she reached over for the lamp on the table, but she knocked it over, and it shattered on the floor.

"Damn it, Bethany!" she called angrily. "Look what happened."

"I'm sorry, Mommy." A deep and distorted voice came from right beside her this time.

Lucile cried out in surprise and jumped back.

"You scared me." She reached out and grasped the girl's wrist before she could make a move to escape.

"Let's go!" She pulled the little girl toward the kitchen. The girl resisted, but only a little.

"You are going to help me clean this up; since it's your fault I broke it."

She pushed open the door and tugged the girl into the kitchen. She flicked on the light and screamed, dropping the girl's arm and falling back onto the floor. She saw the little blonde girl's face—or what was left of it. The girl smiled and giggled, covering up her missing eye. She did a little spin, her bare feet sliding on the polished wooden floor.

"Sorry, Mommy," she heard a little voice above her.

She glanced up, head shaking, and saw the doll with the caved-in face standing on the kitchen counter. She screamed, and covered her head, as if the doll might attack her. Instead, the doll jumped from the countertop, and the little girl caught it in her arms.

"Russell!" Lucile screamed, even though it was no use. He wouldn't hear her. The little girl giggled all the way to the back door, and disappeared outside.

"You are almost there!" Daemon called from the base of the tree. "Almost there."

"Almost there," another little boy repeated; he sat atop the branch Bethany was climbing.

She climbed faster in response to the children's cheers. The boy reached down to help her up.

"There is the hole." He pointed. "Just drop it in, with all the rest of our dolls."

He jumped down from the branch to the one below it.

"I'll see you at the bottom." He smiled at her.

She stretched out her arm toward the hole, but she couldn't reach. She stood up on the branch, leaning against the trunk, pushing herself up on her tiptoes. The children who were sitting on various branches of the tree all jumped down and backed away to get a better look. She hesitated, holding on to the doll at the entrance to the hole. For some reason, she found herself thinking of her father. She pulled her arm back from the hole, looking at the face of the doll, her face.

"Bethany!" She heard her mother's shrill and frightened cries from inside the house.

Bethany closed her eyes and once again outstretched her arm into the darkness of the hole. She felt something inside.

Scales. The snake. She felt its smooth, cold skin coil around her wrist. She let the doll go. She heard it sliding down the hole, deep into the tree. The kids all cheered and applauded from below. She glanced down at Daemon, who nodded his head in proud satisfaction. She returned her attention back to the hole as the snake coiled tighter around her skinny arm. She could only see its yellow glowing eyes staring back at her. She felt a sudden sharp pain as its fangs penetrated her flesh. Then the branch broke.

Bethany didn't even scream, didn't make a sound. Eyes closed, she silently fell down towards the kids' open arms, smiling triumphantly the whole way.

Lucile and Russell searched the house and their surrounding property for Bethany. They didn't find her. Lucile cried hysterically, blaming Russell for allowing their daughter to go play with *those* children.

"My baby ran away!" she screamed over and over again.

They returned home from the search, hoping and praying that their daughter would reappear the next morning. She didn't.

That morning, Russell went outside to search again, and he started with the dead oak tree, only it wasn't so dead. He didn't know how it was possible. No longer rotting, no longer hollowed out. The hole that he had chopped into the tree was gone, as if it had completely healed itself, and little buds on the branches were growing and coming to life.

DEVIL IN THE WOODS

"How long do you think he's been dead?" I asked. My voice was shaky and harsh. My throat burned from all the noise I had made when I almost tripped over the dead man—what was left of him—half-buried in the dry leaves. The smell weighed down the air as putrid particles filled my lungs. I gagged again. I wondered how it was possible I hadn't noticed the awful smell before seeing the body.

"At least a few days," Brad said.

He was down on one knee, examining the gruesome sight. The lower half of the body was covered in the dead leaves. The poor man's face was mostly gone, and his head was unrecognizable and covered in wriggling larvae. His shirt was entirely ripped away. I had the sudden urge to vomit again, but I had emptied my stomach almost immediately after seeing and smelling the corpse. Instead, my whole body convulsed in disgust, yet I was still horrifically mesmerized.

"Maybe longer." He stood up and exhaled loudly. "God, that stinks."

"What do you think got him?" I asked.

I couldn't look away, despite my best effort to move my head. There were several jagged slashes in his chest, but they didn't look like teeth marks.

Claw marks, maybe?

Brad looked over at me and pulled me in with his eyes, and for a few moments, all I could focus on was him and his hypnotic gaze. His eyes were almost surreal; one was so dark it was almost black, the other a pale blue. His mouth didn't move, but his eyes told me what I didn't want to hear. I wanted him to say a bear or a wolf, but the look on his face told me that this was a murder. I shivered, and not from cold. I heard the cry of a raven nearby. It was probably wanting to feast on the dead flesh, impatiently waiting for us to leave.

"Did you bring your gun?" I asked, looking from Brad to the corpse.

I finally noticed that the man's lack of a face was due to part of his skull being caved in.

He nodded. "I always have my gun."

He placed himself in between the corpse and me. "I'd never let anything happen to you, you know that, right?"

"I know." I felt cold, and my skin grew tiny little bumps.

The sun would set soon. The day was warm, but the nightly chill of fall was slowly creeping in.

"What should we do?"

"There's not much we can do right now," he said.

He had his phone out and was taking pictures of the body and the surrounding area. The body rested at the base of a young, skinny tree that was just barely hanging on to its rust-colored leaves. I also noticed a few gray stones protruding from the earth that surrounded us. There were five of them, each only a foot or so high. I did my best to get over my fear, and I tried to make a mental note of the surrounding area. The police would need help finding this place, and any description I could provide might aid them.

"I don't have any service," Brad said, looking at his phone. "We are still a few days from civilization. We can call it in when we get to a town."

"We can't just leave him."

"It's not like we can take him with us."

"Then we should bury him, at least," I argued.

"Then we wouldn't be able to find him when we call it in. That and we shouldn't disturb the crime scene."

I could tell he was getting frustrated. He was trying to keep his cool to prevent me from further freaking out.

"You're right." I was disgusted, horrified, and entranced all at the same time.

I noticed a mark on the man's arm, some sort of symbol. It appeared to be a crescent moon inside a skull, with several little unknown markings around it. I couldn't tell if it was drawn on or tatted, but I didn't want to get close enough to look. He placed a gentle hand on my shoulder and gave me an affectionate scratch.

"Hey, it's going to be okay."

I turned to look up at him. He was literally a foot taller than me, at six feet five. We locked eyes again. He looked almost guilty, as if he felt sorry that I had to witness something so gruesome. He started to pull me in closer, but I turned away from him to start hiking again. I found my legs moving quicker than normal. I suddenly had to be free of the smell before I started gagging again. The putrid odor seemed to stalk us for the next mile.

"I don't think we should build a fire tonight," Brad said, after we set up camp.

Our red tent sat dead center of a small clearing in the trees.

"Call me paranoid, but I don't want to draw too much attention to us."

I nodded. I had already switched to my heavy coat. I sat down on a fallen tree and looked up at the dark blue sky.

"Now I'm wishing we decided to stick to the trail."

"I know what you mean." Brad lit a small lantern. "But don't worry. I told you I'd keep us safe, and I will."

I dug around my pack until I found a bag of jerky. I inhaled the sweet smell and took a piece of meat before offering the bag.

"I wonder why," I said, taking a bird-bite of jerky. I wasn't hungry, despite my empty stomach.

"Why what?"

"Why would someone just carve into someone like that? Smash their skull? Kill them?"

"There's no understanding psychopaths," he said. "Their brains don't work the same way ours do."

I thought about that for a while, and then nodded my head.

"I'm getting kind of tir—" My voice lost sound when I heard the sharp snap of a stick nearby.

Brad was on his feet in a heartbeat, holding up the lantern to see. The wind immediately picked up, dragging leaves across the ground. A sudden chill ripped through my entire body, and I had a single violent shiver.

"I don't see anything," he said, taking a few steps toward the trees.

My eyes followed him as he moved farther away from me. I had the sudden uncanny feeling that eyes were burning into me, and not from just one direction. The forest seemed to come alive, and I was suddenly aware of everything around me, every move of a branch being brushed by the wind, every leaf scraping against the ground, the buzz of every bug flying in the cold air.

"Do you see anything?" I called.

As if in response to my voice, something shot out from between the trees by where Brad stood, and ran deeply into the darkness. I jumped off the ground ready to run like hell, heart pounding, blood rushing.

My skin suddenly felt hot despite the cold.

"I think it was just a deer!" Brad called. "I couldn't get a good look."

I sighed heavily and forced a chuckle.

"I feel like I'm going to jump at every sound and shadow," I admitted.

"I think we will both be on edge for a while," he said as he returned to me, lantern lowered.

"But whoever the murderer was, he should be days away from us now. I wouldn't worry, babe."

Babe. He hadn't called me babe in a while. I guess that meant he thought things were back to normal. He sat down beside me and placed an arm around my shoulder. I immediately stood back up.

"I need to take a piss," I said and hurried away into the dark.

I didn't really have to pee, and I'm positive that Brad was aware that I just needed an escape. I knew he would have that all-too-familiar defeated look on his face, but I didn't care. I kept walking through the trees until the light of his lantern dimmed. I sighed and leaned back against the thick trunk of a pine tree. My hands clenched and unclenched and clenched again.

Meredith, with her long dark hair, olive skin, and chocolate eyes, invaded my thoughts. I saw her smiling face, and then her crying face.

I forced myself to look up at the stars and inhaled

the scent of pine. I had never seen so many stars in my life before hiking out here, and I lost myself in the twinkling lights. Meredith's face faded from my mind and eventually my anger faded along with it, but new grief settled in.

Things between Brad and me would never be the same. As my attention returned to the woods, my eyes noticed a new glow in the distance. It was a campfire. It was rare to run into another group of hikers this deep into the woods, days away from the nearest path or town. The glow was far off, at least a mile or so.

An eerie gut feeling inside told me that we shouldn't go over there to investigate. It could have been the crazy, murdering psychopath. I ignored the glow, and I walked back to camp. I found Brad sitting right where I left him. He watched me silently as I approached. I could feel the frustrated and desperate energy seeping out of him. He wanted so badly for me to just get over it, to love him the same way I had. That was never going to happen. I stopped a few feet from him and crossed my arms over my chest. He knew why I fled. He knew why I did my best to avoid his touch. I'd been dodging his embrace for a while.

"You're going to have to forgive me at some point," he said, after the silence grew uncomfortable. His legs were sprawled out and he wasn't looking at me anymore; instead, he stared at his hiking boots.

"I mean, this trip was supposed to be about us getting back on track. Just you and me, the trees, and the stars."

"I'm glad we came," I said.

His head rose, and his eyes met mine. I loved his eyes, and I hated that I loved his eyes. I forced a smile.

"Despite the corpse in the woods, this trip was just what we needed."

"That definitely dampened things a bit," he said seriously. He motioned for me to sit beside him. I didn't move.

"Casey, we've been out here for three days, and you've done nothing but push me away."

He sounded so sad—whiny even, like he was going to cry. I'd never seen him cry in the several years I'd known him.

"I'm so, so incredibly sorry."

"I know," I said. "You've said it before, and if you keep saying it, it's only going to bring back the angry feeling, so just drop it already. I'm here. I showed up. You have me where you want me, and you know how I feel about you."

He sat forward and rested his hands on his knees.

"You are the one I want. The only one I will ever want."

I exhaled slowly.

"Let's go to bed," I said, nodding toward the tent. "Maybe I'll even let you cuddle me tonight."

He smiled at that. Then he stood up and brushed himself off. I walked over to the tent, and he followed close behind.

I awoke in the middle of the night to a shrill scream in the distance. At first I thought I had only dreamed the sound. I couldn't fully remember my dream, other than a few fragmented images of the dead body. Sleep was no escape; the image would stick with me forever. I closed my eyes to try to drift back off, but I heard the sound a second time. It was definitely a woman's scream. I grasped Brad's hand on my belly and shook it.

"Wake up," I called. It took several calls of his name to get a response.

"What's wrong?" he asked, only half awake.

"Just listen," I said quietly.

We both listened to the wind for what felt like forever.

"I heard a scream," I said finally. "A woman's scream."

"You were just dreaming, babe," he said, clutching me closer, sliding his fingers across my stomach. He kissed the back of my neck.

"Seriously, it was …" I stopped speaking when we both heard the shrill, almost inhuman, scream of pain in the distance. Brad shot up and scrambled for his clothes. I followed suit.

"I saw a campfire," I admitted. "Earlier tonight."

"And you are telling me this now?" He moved outside the tent. "Christ, Casey, why didn't you say something?"

"I didn't want you to go look," I said, right behind him.

He tucked his gun into his jeans. "Where did you see it?" His tone was furious.

"This way," I said, moving toward the trees.

The last thing I wanted to do was to go investigate the

scream, but leaving someone obviously suffering and in pain seemed wrong.

"I'm sorry, I was just … afraid."

He said nothing. He lit a lantern as we walked. The glow of the distant campfire was gone, but I knew we were headed in the right direction.

"I can't believe you didn't tell me," he snapped.

"So you could what? Go investigate? You're not a cop."

"We could have warned them."

"Or it could have been the murderer," I said.

It was so odd talking about someone in that context in real life—an actual murderer lurking around the woods—and Brad and I were running to the rescue.

"This is so stupid, Brad; we should be looking out for ourselves."

"When we get there, you are going to hide while I go look."

"I'm not leaving you."

"Damn it, Case, just once do what the fuck I tell you to do!"

I didn't dare argue or even respond. I just hurried along beside him. There was no reasoning with him once he got like that. He was angry and determined; he probably thought he could even save someone. There was another shrill, desperate, horrified cry of pain from just up ahead. It stopped us both in our tracks, and I found my hands coming up and covering my own mouth.

Brad extended his arm to the side, blocking me from moving any farther. He blew out the lantern, and I knelt down behind a tree. I saw that he already had his gun drawn. He moved quickly without making a sound. I inched closer, wanting to see. My eyes were still adjusting to the darkness. I wasn't sure how far ahead Brad had moved.

Despite hiding, I felt completely exposed without him near me. I couldn't see much up ahead, so I sat and listened. Brad was an idiot for going off on his own, playing detective. I hoped he would be okay. I also hoped he could save whoever it was that was screaming, but I knew she would already be dead. That last scream we heard, it was a last scream. You'd never know what such a thing sounds like until you've heard it.

Again, the entire forest around me seemed to move. The hair on my neck stiffened, as I suddenly felt like there were eyes on me. Many eyes. The trees seemed busy now. Branches moved with what must have been the wind. I heard a faraway howl of a wild dog or wolf somewhere behind, back from the direction we had come.

I wanted Brad to come back. I didn't want to be alone in the woods. I didn't know what I expected to come after me: a psycho with a knife, a wolf, or something else. I shivered violently as the wind grew stronger, but it wasn't just the wind I heard. There were other sounds with it. Words, even.

Whispers.

I heard whispers on the wind, low tones talking so fast and quietly I couldn't understand a word. But the sounds were words, I'm sure of it. The whispers seemed to come from all around me. I looked up at the stars and at the full moon that peeked through the trees. It was odd; I could have sworn that last night the moon had only been half full. Maybe I was just going crazy due to the stress.

I shut it all out. I was trying to focus on anything other than the moon, the movement, and the noise in the night. I knew my head was playing games with itself. I waited and tried to steady my breathing.

The sky above me suddenly darkened. The moon disappeared behind a cloud. As the darkness consumed me, everything suddenly became silent. The trees stopped. The wind stopped. The whispers stopped. After several seconds, I realized I was holding my breath.

In the dark stillness, I heard a single sound, a low growl. My chest burned when my heart missed a beat. I quickly realized that the moon wasn't behind a cloud. The moonlight was blocked by someone standing over me. I cried out and bolted from behind the tree. It was too dark for me to tell who it was, but he was tall, very tall, and I think he wore a hood over his head. I looked back as I zigzagged through the trees, but whoever it was wasn't there anymore.

I sprinted in the direction Brad had went, while cursing under my breath at the fact that he left me in the first place. I glanced back again to make sure I wasn't being followed, and panic forced my legs to keep moving. The hooded figure was standing right behind me.

Standing.

In the split second that my head was turned, the figure didn't seem to be moving at all. He wasn't running. He was standing. I picked up speed in panic and looked behind me. There he was again, just a few feet behind, standing still. He wore a cloak that covered him from head to toe. His arms hung firmly at his sides. He wasn't moving, yet he was behind me. I kept running until I burst through a clearing in the trees.

"Brad!" I called as I tripped over a tree root and fell hard on the ground, rolling across the dirt and leaves.

The fall knocked the wind out of me, and I coughed as I scrambled across the dirt to my feet. I looked behind me, waiting for the hooded man to emerge from the trees. I covered my mouth with my hands to muffle the scream. I had run right under him.

Hanging there by the neck, swaying back and forth, a human body dangled from the thick branch of a tree. I could feel wetness in my eyes. I clasped my hands so tightly together, they ached. I prayed it wasn't Brad. I couldn't breathe as I inched closer to it.

"Casey." I heard my name behind me.

I turned and latched onto him and rested my head against his solid frame. He held me tightly, and I instantly felt warm again.

"I saw something, in the woods. A man. He was chasing after me."

Brad continued to hold me. He kissed my head and pulled me farther into the clearing.

"I'll never leave you again, okay. I promise."

He kept glancing into the trees, as if he expected the mystery man to appear.

"We'll stay together."

"Did you find the girl?" I asked, pulling away.

I looked around the campsite and saw a mangled tent. There were tears all along its side revealing the mess of clothes inside, and their supplies were scattered across the campground.

"I didn't find the screaming girl," he said.

I didn't like the way he said it.

"Clarify."

He motioned for me to follow him. This time the smell did hit me before I saw the body. I didn't want to look. Instead, I grabbed Brad and buried my head into his chest again.

"You said you saw a fire here?" Brad asked.

I nodded. "Yeah, why?"

"I don't think the light you saw could have been a fire." He motioned to a makeshift fire pit in the center of the campsite. "There's no embers. I think it's been a while since this fire pit was used. And that body over there, she's been dead a few days. They've both been dead awhile. Maybe almost as long as the first body we saw."

"Then who was screaming?"

"I'm not sure," he said. "I couldn't find anyone, or even hear anything when I got here. I searched all over this place."

"I can't take this, Brad," I said. "I want to get away from here. I want to go home." I couldn't tell if I was shaking from the cold, or from fear.

"You can't lose it," he said seriously. "Listen to me, Case …" He placed his hands on both of my cheeks and forced me to meet his gaze. "I'm going to get us out of here, but it's going to take time. We probably have almost three days ahead of us before we make it to the next town. We just have to be careful and keep moving."

"Well, let's get moving," I said, after a long pause.

"We have to go back to our camp to grab our things," he said. "We'd never make it without our gear."

"I'm not going back there, not now." I pulled away from him. "He's back there."

"We have to."

"Let's just wait it out til morning, then," I said. "Sunrise is only a few hours away. We can stay here until then."

"If that's what you want, we'll stay here." He didn't seem disappointed about it.

The last thing either of us wanted was to be ambushed while moving through the trees. At least in this clearing, we would see him before he got to us. We sat in the center of the campsite by the unlit fire pit and waited. The smell was nauseating, but I'd rather have dealt with that than face the woods at night with that hooded man lurking about.

I rested my head in Brad's lap and tried to relax. He gently scratched my head. Despite fear and anxiety, I fell asleep after a while.

I opened my eyes at first light, but when I awoke, my head wasn't in Brad's lap. Instead, it rested on the hard ground. I sat up with a groan. My neck was sore from sleeping at an odd angle.

"Brad!" I called, looking around the campsite.

A loud crunching sound made me jump. The sound came from the far end of the clearing where the woman's body had been. Brad was there, in his red jacket, his hood over his head. He was on his knees beside the body. His back was to me.

What was he doing? Was he touching it?

I heard more loud crunching, a crunching sound that reminded me of a dog destroying a bone.

"Brad," I called softly as I slowly walked over to him.

His head was hung low over the woman's corpse. From that close, the smell would have been sickening.

"Brad," I called, louder this time. He froze. The crunching stopped. He didn't move an inch as I moved closer. "What are you doing?"

I heard a low growl, and he slowly turned his head to face me. I screamed when I saw his face—not Brad's face, and not quite a human face, either.

Its eyes were black with red slits, its skin a pale beige and rubbery, and its long hair was grey and thinning. In less than a second, my back was slamming against the ground, and its fangs were snapping in my face.

I woke up to Brad calling my name and shaking me.

"It's time to get moving."

I sighed in relief, realizing I had been asleep. He looked down at me, and his expression turned worried.

"Are you okay?"

"Just a nightmare," I said.

I couldn't get rid of the crunching sound in my head, the sound of human bones being crushed under teeth. He helped me up. We looked around the campsite for anything useful, a radio, a weapon, food. We found nothing.

In the daylight, I could clearly see the two corpses. The woman was probably in her forties, with long, jet-black hair. Her eyes were practically bulging from her head due to decomposition. The man hanging from the tree was older than her. Neither body wore any clothes.

Brad caught me staring at the dangling man and came up behind me. He had to physically turn me away to snap me out of the trance.

"That's not going to happen to you," he said. "I won't let it."

I believed him. I wanted to talk to him about the weird symbol on the woman's arm, the crescent moon and skull. At first, I thought it was a tattoo, but it was drawn on in blood that had dried and caked over. The man didn't have the mark on his arm, and I wondered why. For some reason, I couldn't find my voice. I couldn't bring myself to ask Brad about his theories. Instead, he held my hand tightly and pulled me along into the trees.

We took a roundabout way to the campsite, not wanting to risk finding the hooded man, although he was hopefully long gone by now. We walked in silence. As we rose in elevation, my legs grew tired.

I kept glancing around behind me to make sure we weren't being followed. The woods looked peaceful. Birds were chirping, warm sun beamed down on us. Two hours went by, and we still hadn't made it back to the campsite.

"Shouldn't we have made it back by now?" I asked.

"I was just thinking the same thing," he said, stopping. "Shit. I'm sorry, I'm normally really good at this." He was clearly frustrated.

"You are, but you're stressed," I said, trying to support him. "So am I. It should be around here somewhere. Maybe we just curved around too far and passed it."

"Let's backtrack," he suggested. "We aren't moving uphill anymore, so it can't be too far."

We did our best to retrace our steps to find a familiar point. Every tree started to look the same to me, and the birds seemed to be repeating their same songs over and over again. Fear and stress were getting to me. I wanted to be free of the woods, but running around looking for our gear wasn't getting us any closer to escaping the woodland prison.

After walking in panicked silence for another hour, I heard a new sound. Ravens were cawing.

"No fucking way," I said.

The smell hit me this time, and I didn't even have to look at the man's body, half-buried in the dry leaves. The blackbirds flew up from the corpse, cursing us for disturbing their meal.

"This can't be happening; this can't be happening," I repeated over and over.

Brad grabbed my shoulders tight and gave me a gentle shake. "Hey, calm down. We must have passed our campsite by about a mile, that's it. Now we know exactly where we are."

"But …"

"Stop—you're panicking. I can't have you panicking. I know you never want to see a dead body again, but this is actually a good thing. I can get us back to camp now. I promise."

I nodded. He was so confident, and it helped. He could protect us. I knew he could.

"Come on, let's hurry. I could really use some water and maybe some food."

He tugged my hand, and I followed him at a jog. It didn't take long. Brad had been right; camp was just over a mile away, but when we got there, he let out a cry of disbelief and anger. His tent was caved in, and the sides were torn to ribbons. Clothes were ripped and scattered around the campsite.

"Son of a bitch!" he yelled.

The anger in his voice only added to my distress.

"Find your phone," I said softly. I didn't think he heard me, but he immediately went searching through the mess. "We probably won't have service, but they might still be able to track us if we call 911."

I moved to the tent and started searching through our belongings. I was trying to be optimistic, but I knew waiting for help could take just as long as escaping the woods.

"Hey!" he called.

I looked out from a hole in the torn walls of the tent.

"Your pack is still here," he said, lifting the black bag. "It's sitting where you were last night. Everything seems to be in it."

"Did you find my phone?"

"Yeah, but I think you forgot to turn it off because it's dead."

"No way," I said, hurrying over. "I turned my phone off before we even left the car."

"It doesn't look like you did," he snapped.

He glared at me with his dark eye. I didn't say anything. I felt defeated and helpless. Brad must have realized his anger wasn't helping the situation, because his voice softened.

"My sleeping bag is ruined, but we still have yours. And you have some food in here, too."

"And the knife," I said, when I saw him hold up the black case containing the blade.

I took it from him and clipped it onto my belt. Brad moved to the tent and frantically searched for useful things. I found his water bottle outside the tent. It had been emptied out, but I put it in the side pocket of my backpack.

"Do you think you can track whoever did this?" I asked.

I looked over at Brad through the hole in the tent and saw him put something in his jacket pocket.

"Or get an idea of what direction they went, so we can move in the opposite?"

"I think you guys are in luck," a man's voice called from the trees.

Brad whipped out his pistol and moved from the tent to my side. "Who the hell are you?" he demanded.

"Whoa … easy, killer," he said, holding his hands up in the air. He was much older than us, in his late forties, early fifties. His beard was graying, and he wore a red and black flannel shirt over blue jeans. His hair was tucked back into a red hunting cap.

"I'm not here to hurt you."

"What are you doing here?" Brad called.

"The name's Mort. I'm just here hiking like the two of you." He motioned to his pack on his shoulders. "With all the screaming and yelling, I figured I should come check things out. See if anyone needed help."

"We're fine," Brad said.

"Doesn't look like it to me," he said. "Looks like you two need all the help you can get."

"Do you have a phone or radio?" I asked.

"I do back at the cabin," he said. "It's a ways away, a little over a day. No roads go to it or anything, it's really secluded. I've been hiking for a few days, I do loops around the area."

"You live out here?" I asked.

Brad eyed me with annoyance. I shrugged, not knowing what else to do besides keep the conversation going.

"I come out here for summer and fall, head back to town in the winter. Now can you please lower your gun already? If I wanted to kill you, I'd have shot you when I saw you."

Brad looked to me for approval. I nodded. Brad slowly lowered his pistol, but he didn't put it away.

"Mort, there's been a murder out here," I said. "A few of them, actually."

"I reckon girls don't scream for dear life in the middle of the night for much else," he said. "It's unfortunate, though. I heard it last night, faintly, from where I was camping. No chance of me getting there in time."

He knelt down and examined something in the dirt.

"Whoever ransacked your camp went that way," he pointed behind him with his thumb. "You can see for yourself, there's fresh tracks that I imagine don't match any of ours."

His lack of emotion in response to the murder made me a little uneasy.

"I still don't trust him," Brad said to me, as if Mort wasn't standing right there.

"Whoever I met last night was a lot taller than him," I said. Despite my rationalizing, I didn't trust him either.

"Come on," he said. "You can come back to my cabin and meet my woman; she'll be there. She can make you a nice meal, too."

Brad didn't move.

"I don't think we are in a position to deny help," I

said, touching his arm and giving it a gentle squeeze.

Mort gave us an odd look. I walked over to my pack and picked it up. Brad took it from me and threw it on his back.

"Are you sure about this?"

"No," I said. "But I don't think he wants to hurt us."

"If he tries anything …"

"I know," I said. I forced a half smile. "Let's get moving. If whoever destroyed our stuff is headed that way, I want to be going in just about any other direction."

Mort led the way through the trees. We walked for hours without a break. My legs were sore, but I didn't dare ask to stop. I was almost out of water; I had been sharing with Brad all day. We would have to find some soon.

"There's a river not too far from here," Mort said, somehow knowing that our water supply was running low. "It's going to take us longer to get to the cabin, but we should probably head that way first. We can camp out by the river and make it to the cabin by dinnertime tomorrow."

I still didn't trust Mort, but at the same time, I was kind of relieved to have a third person around. I didn't know how he did it; wandering the woods alone would terrify me. I kept looking over at Brad. He had the most focused expression on his face. I swear his eyes never left Mort. Brad probably suspected the old man was leading us to our death.

It took several hours to make it to the river, but when we did, I had to stop and stare at the beauty of it all.

The sound of water rushing, the pink hue of the sky at sunset. It was almost enough to make me forget the horror we had faced. Mort rested on a log while Brad and I went down to the river to refill our bottles.

"He doesn't seem so dangerous," I said.

Brad didn't respond. He knelt down to dip his bottle in the river. I looked out across the water at the other side and couldn't see anything but trees. I stooped down behind him and massaged his shoulders. After several seconds, I could feel him relax.

"Funny how last night you were the one talking me down. Today it's the opposite."

I kissed the back of his neck. He reached a hand over his shoulder and grasped mine.

"I would feel safer if it were just the two of us," he said quietly.

"I know. We'll keep an eye on him, sleep in shifts or something."

"You can sleep first."

"You hardly got any last night," I said. "I'll stay awake first."

"Case …"

"What's the first thing you are going to do when we get home?" I asked, interrupting him to change the subject.

"Probably sleep forever, or at least two days."

"I think I'm going to take the longest shower of my life," I said. "And then down a bottle of wine, maybe two."

"You still have the ice wine I bought you. It's in the fridge."

"I almost forgot," I said.

Ice wine was like sweet heaven in a glass. He had bought me an expensive bottle from Germany, along with flowers, as part of his pathetic apology for betraying my trust. Then my fall break from college came and he suggested we just drop everything and leave for a two-week trip to the woods. We went on a major hike every year, and this year I chose the route. I wished I had let him choose.

"We should probably get back to our guest," I said, after a long pause.

"Let's just stay here a while," he said tightening his grip on my hand.

I sighed and obeyed. I sat down beside him and watched the water run. He scratched my back, and I lay my head on his shoulder. I closed my eyes, and all I could see was Meredith's bitch face. I couldn't help but imagine the two of them rolling around together.

"Are you okay?" he asked me, kissing the top of my head. "You're shaking."

"Just a little cold," I lied. "But you're warming me up."

Meredith had apologized at least ten times, left me voicemails, and sent me a book-long text message blaming everything on the alcohol. I ignored my best friend of seventeen years, and planned to continue to do so.

"Drink?" We both heard Mort's voice behind us.

I turned to face him and he held out a large silver flask. Brad eyed him but didn't move. I took the flask and drank. Smooth scotch slid down my throat. I hated dark liquors, but Brad loved them.

"This is right up your alley," I said, holding it up to Brad to smell.

He took it and drank.

"Good, huh?" Mort asked.

Brad handed me the flask to give back to Mort.

"So how long have you two, uh …" he paused and took a swig. "… been together?"

"Three years," Brad answered before I could. He was staring across the river. "But we've known each other since high school. Casey got me through some pretty tough times." I knew those words were more for me than they were for Mort.

A tinge of guilt hit me, and I wasn't sure why. I had nothing to feel guilty about. He was the one who fucked everything up after we'd been through so many rough years. His family literally hated him. hated me, too. Back in high school, he struggled through drugs, thugs, and depression, and I was by his side every step of the way, until he finally got his shit together.

I went on to college, and he came to live with me and helped pay rent on our off-campus apartment. That's when we started officially dating. He went to trade school and got a good job, while I studied for my pre-law degree.

"I see …" Mort said before taking another drink. "Well, good luck to the both of ya. We'll get you out of these woods."

"Do murders happen around here often?" I asked. "You just seem so calm about it all."

"Murders happen everywhere often," Mort said. "Seems like everywhere you go, you run into death. No escaping it, not even out here in the peace of the wilds."

"How long have you been coming out here?" Brad asked. One drink was all it took for his tone to warm up.

"At least forty years," he said. "That cabin has been in my family for ages. Leftover from the old days. These woods, though, there's something special about 'em."

"How so?" I asked.

"Just spend some time here," he said. "And you'll see. You'll never leave."

His words brought a sudden chill to the air, and I swear I could suddenly see fog in my breath.

"I'm going to go start a fire," Mort said and got up. He held out the flask to us. "You can finish that off."

I took it and watched as he headed off toward camp. I found myself grateful for his exit. I passed the flask to Brad without taking a drink. He took another swig without hesitation.

"I really hope things can get back to normal with us," he said after a long pause.

He was rolling the flask around in his hands.

"They will," I said, with enough sincerity to almost lie to myself.

I wanted it to, wished I could turn back the past and lead us in a different direction.

"We should get back to set up camp," I said, standing.

When we found Mort, he was stacking sticks together in a pit that he had built.

"Do you think it's a good idea to start a fire?" I asked. "What if … he finds us?"

"He'll find you either way," Mort said.

"What do you mean by that?" Brad demanded; his tone had returned to threatening. I noticed his hand moved to his gun at his waist, but he didn't pull it out.

"Exactly what I said." Mort looked over at us, straight-faced and impassive. "He's been here a lot longer than all of us. He'll be here long after us."

"You know the killer?"

Mort's voice was low. "I'm afraid it ain't that simple," he said.

Mort's eyes suddenly looked completely black. His face lost all color until it became gray, and the skin on his cheeks sagged. He grinned a toothy grin and a thick, black liquid dripped from the sides of his mouth. I screamed and jumped back. Brad looked over at me, startled and confused. I looked from him to Mort, whose skin and eyes were back to normal. The look on Mort's face was equally perplexed.

"What is it?" Brad asked, pistol out and looking around at the trees, expecting to see someone, anything that might have caused me to lose it.

"I …" *Did he not see it? Was I going crazy? Had I imagined the whole thing?*

My head was spinning, and I found myself on my knees. There was a sudden throbbing pain in my head, centered right behind my eyes. "It's fine."

"Case, are you all right?" Brad asked, concerned. He was rubbing my back while giving Mort a warning glance to stay back.

"These woods, they have a way of screwing with you," Mort said. "I tell you what, this place has a mind of its own."

"What did you mean, he'd find us either way?" Brad demanded, his hands still on me. "Who the hell is he, and how do you know him?"

"It's a legend, really," Mort said. "But a story is always different, depending on who tells it. My grandmother told me all about an evil witch who chews on the souls of the dead, and who can appear as any one of its victims. It's forever bound to this forest, and will do anything to be free of its chains. My wife knows about that story, but she talks about a spirit who watches over the forest. She says that whoever dies here can live on in the forest forever."

"Never mind! I don't care," Brad interrupted loudly.

He turned his attention fully to me. He must have immediately written Mort off as a superstitious nut.

"What happened with you?" he asked.

"Nothing," I said. I didn't want to tell him what I saw. I didn't believe what I saw, yet I knew I had seen it.

"I just thought I saw something, but it was nothing."

"Don't scare me like that," he said, helping me up.

I looked at Mort, who was back to setting up wood for a fire. Brad and I didn't question him about it again. We just left him to his business.

I sat beside Brad in front of the fire opposite Mort. Several times he caught me staring at him. I was watching him closely, waiting for his face to change again. Brad was looking really tired, but judging from the determined look on his face, he wasn't going to allow himself to sleep anytime soon.

The cold crept in with the darkness, and I shivered. Brad noticed and put his arm around my shoulders. Mort surprised us with a second flask and took a swig. He tossed it over the fire and, despite his sleepy eyes, Brad caught it with one hand. He offered it to me first, but I declined. He took a long drink.

"Tomorrow at the cabin, you can radio in what you saw," Mort said. "The murders. Such a shame."

"Thanks," Brad muttered.

"I'm curious about this legend you spoke of earlier," I said, "You think the man I saw in the woods is connected to it?"

I could feel Brad's irritation rise immediately with my question. His hand tightened on my shoulder. I could feel his nails digging into me through my jacket. The fire reflected off Mort's eyes as he stared into mine, and it took him a long time to speak.

"The way my grandmother put it, the woods are his. He's bound to them, and he can never leave. So, he doesn't want anyone else to leave, either." He closed his eyes and nodded his head, as if agreeing with himself. "But don't worry, he ain't gonna kill ya."

"And what does your wife say about this forest spirit?" I asked.

"That's enough," Brad said before Mort could answer. He tossed the flask back across the fire.

"I've heard enough." I don't think Brad could have held me any tighter to himself. "I don't care about your legends. I just want to get the hell out of here and never look back."

I looked up at Brad but didn't say anything. The look on his face almost frightened me, and he suddenly seemed hot to the touch. Mort was silent. He took another sip from his flask. I didn't dare ask another question. Instead, I curled up to Brad's warmth and closed my eyes. I fell asleep quickly, but not deeply. Instead, I dropped into that shallow sleep where your brain uncontrollably wanders, and random images and words flow through your mind.

I kept seeing Meredith's long dark hair, her smile. I kept seeing Mort's face, his other face, the dead face. I also saw Brad's face, his charming smirk as he lowered his lips to mine. The kiss was short, wet. As he pulled away, I saw his face again, almost unrecognizable as part of his head was bashed in and blood oozed over every inch of his flesh.

Startled, I awoke. The fire was out except for the last few glowing embers. Brad was lying down beside me, still clutching me to him. I didn't remember moving. It felt like I had only been asleep for a minute. I looked across the camp, and I couldn't see Mort anywhere.

Did he leave? Had Brad offended him and sent him off into the woods?

I didn't know whether I was relieved or frightened to be alone again. I was glad that Brad was finally able to sleep, though. I gripped his arm and gently lifted it off of me as I sat up.

"Hey," he called softly. His eyes opened.

"Everything's fine," I whispered. "I'll be right back,"

I kissed his cheek. He turned his head and kissed me on the lips. I started to pull away, but for some reason, I stopped myself. I kissed him back, really kissed him. He tasted of scotch. His arms wrapped around my waist, and his mouth moved to my neck. He nibbled on my skin. An image of his caved-in face invaded my mind, and I finally stopped him.

"I really need to go pee," I said, giggling. "I'll be right back though, babe."

He smiled and closed his eyes.

I stood up and eyed the entire campsite. Sure enough, Mort and all of his belongings were nowhere to be found. I moved to the trees to take a piss. When I finished, I looked up at the moon and stars again. I was stalling. I missed Brad so much, desperately wished I could take back the past. I couldn't. What was done was done.

After daydreaming, I realized how busy the forest seemed. How loud the air was. The forest was whispering again. I tried to focus on the sounds, tried to single out a voice from the hundreds. Finally, something in midst of the rustling of voices spoke to me, clear and close.

"Run."

I'm sure that's what it said. When the single word was spoke, all was silent. Eerily quiet. I recognized the silence.

Panic set in, and as I turned to move back to Brad, there he was — the tall, dark figure. I think the cloak he wore was made of black feathers, and like the reaper himself, the cloak covered him from head to toe. It was too dark to see his face through the hood over his head. He stood in front of me, unmoving amongst the trees.

I tried to cry out, but no sound escaped my mouth. I turned away from the thing and froze. Brad was standing, staring at me. In the light of the moon, I saw him clearly. A twisted smile crossed his face. At his feet lay a body. I covered my mouth with my hands. It was my body. I was sleeping at his feet.

But how was that possible?

That's when I noticed the huge rock in Brad's hands. I don't think it was there before. He lifted it up over his head, and he dropped it over mine. I cried out into the night and sat up, gasping for air. My heart was bursting against my ribcage with each pump. I was struggling to breathe.

Why couldn't I breathe?

"Hey," Brad called from beside me. He sat up and placed an arm around me.

"It's okay, it was just a dream."

He kissed me and pulled me to him.

"I'm right here."

He kissed my head again several times and forced me to look at him.

"I've got you. Nothing's going to happen to you."

I slowed my breathing, inhaling and exhaling deeply. I felt like jelly in his arms. He pulled my head down to his chest and held me tightly. It had been the most vivid dream sequence of my life. I could have sworn I had been awake. Hell, I could still taste Brad's scotch breath.

"Everything okay?" Mort's voice came from across the campsite. I guess I had only dreamed that he left.

"We're fine," Brad said.

"Just trying to help. Need some water?"

"We're fine," Brad said louder.

"Scotch," I called pulling away from Brad, and turning to him. Mort was sitting up in his sleeping bag. The fire was mostly out, but a few last glowing logs illuminated his face.

"Got any more?"

I couldn't fall back asleep. Even after Brad and Mort were both sound asleep, I just sat there. I couldn't erase the vivid dream from my mind. I couldn't unsee Brad crushing my head with a rock, or that twisted smile. I couldn't unsee Mort's dead face. I couldn't understand what was happening to me or why

I was the only one who seemed to be affected, the only one who seemed really afraid.

What did Mort know?

When the sun rose, I woke them both up.

"It's time to start moving," I said, determined. "I want out of these woods."

We refilled our water bottles one more time before heading out.

Mort led the way, Brad in the middle. Without using his words, Brad insisted that he stay in between us. It was as if he knew Mort was a real threat to me. That, or maybe Brad just didn't want me to ask Mort any more questions. I couldn't help it, but I found myself unable to fully trust Brad in a brand-new way. I wanted to believe he would protect me, and I was almost certain he would. But something about that dream followed me through the forest.

I looked at the ground as we walked, careful not to trip over any tree roots or rocks. My legs were getting tired again, and I was getting hungry, but I didn't want to stop. All I could think about was being home in bed, wanting to forget everything that had happened. I heard the cry of a raven nearby. I looked up in the trees for it, but couldn't find it.

When my eyes returned to the ground, I cried out, "Brad!"

There was a second shadow of a person walking right beside me, just to my right. I spun all the way around, looking for someone else. No one stood beside me. When I looked back at the ground, the shadow was gone.

"What is it?" Brad asked.

"Um, let's take a break," I said, ignoring the fact that I was, indeed, losing my mind. "Drink some water. God, I wish I had some vodka right now."

We walked for miles before the trees started to get closer together, so close that their dead branches started to twist around each other. The dry leaves on the ground were piled high, well above my ankles.

"Whoa!" I called.

Both Brad and Mort walked right past it without noticing. I stopped by a tree and reached out and slid my fingers across four deep cuts in the bark. They looked oddly similar to the slash marks on the dead bodies. The spacing between gashes was almost exact. On the tree, it looked like claw marks. I looked around and noticed several other marks on nearby trees. The marks led forward.

"What the hell is that?" Brad asked, more to himself than to me. "A bear, maybe?"

"Beats me," I said. "But I don't like that the marks are in the direction we are walking."

"I don't think they are fresh," Mort chimed in. "I've seen marks like those before. There's some big critters running around here. We aren't that far, though; we should keep moving."

I turned to Mort and stared at him a long time, so long that he began to look uncomfortable. Brad noticed it, too. He placed a hand on my back to get me to budge ,and I snapped out of an almost trancelike state.

"Sorry," I muttered. I placed a hand at my belt to make sure that I still had my knife. "Let's go."

We trekked along for another hour and a half through the thick trees until we finally came to a clearing. If I hadn't been so mentally distressed, I would have probably thought the place was beautiful.

A small wooden cabin, half-covered in moss, sat in the center of a purple flower-covered meadow. Somehow, the flowers managed to survive this late into fall. The cabin looked old, but well-kept. A long deck stretched across the entire front of the cabin.

"You live here?" Brad asked, his tone lighthearted.

"Half the year," Mort said proudly. "One of the most remote homes you could ever find."

"This is pretty awesome, actually," Brad said.

He turned to me and smiled, a real smile. I forced one back. We followed Mort up the wooden steps to the front door of the cabin. The steps were old and creaky. Mort pushed open the door and entered. Brad followed. I hesitated, glancing around the property. Instead of following inside, I walked to the far end of the porch and looked around the side of the cabin. I noticed a double wooden door, chained shut, which must have led down to the cellar. My eyes looked past the cellar to the far side of the house.

I saw a face peeking around the side, relatively low

to the ground. In less than a second, whoever it was, retreated out of sight. I was sure that it was a little boy's face.

"Hey!" I called out.

I hoped over the porch rail and dropped to the ground below. I half-walked, half-jogged along the side of the house, past the cellar, to the far end of the cabin. I poked my head around and saw nothing but flowers and a wooden outhouse. I moved to turn the corner, but I was grabbed by the hand and yanked back around. I looked into Brad's eyes.

"Hey, are you okay? I called to you, but you didn't seem to hear me."

"I'm fine, but I think I just saw a boy." I looked past Brad to Mort, who was standing a few feet behind him. "Do you have a son?"

Mort shook his head, but didn't say anything. Even from that far, I could see his facial expression change. He looked uncomfortable. Worried, even.

"My wife's not here," he called. "I'm gonna go look for her. She's probably close by. She likes to find a spot near the trees to read. Feel free to make yourselves comfortable." He turned and headed into the meadow.

Brad continued holding my hand, and led me back around the side of the cabin to the front door.

"Mort said the radio is in the back room," he said, once we entered.

The cabin seemed bigger on the inside than it did from the outside. The front room was simple, and every piece of furniture appeared handmade. There was a simple wooden table with three chairs, a long wooden bench with red handwoven cushions covering it that made a couch, and a fireplace made of small stones.

"I'll see if I can get the radio working. Mort says they have plenty of food, if you want to grab some."

Brad brought my hand up to his mouth and kissed it before walking down a narrow hallway that led to two back rooms, probably bedrooms.

There was a doorway that opened up to the kitchen. I noticed right away that there wasn't a refrigerator, but there were many cabinets, a large pantry for dry goods, and a wood-fired oven. I opened the pantry. The walls were lined with bagged and canned goods. I examined the shelves, spotting several mason jars filled with what appeared to be different types of chili and stew. I grabbed a jar of what looked like chicken chili. I spotted several types of dark beans in the jar.

"This will do," I said aloud, and turned to exit the pantry.

The jar fell from my hands and shattered on the wooden floor as I jumped. There was a noise below me, and the floorboards under my feet were pushed upward. I heard feet scurry away below me and the sound of what might have been a low giggle.

Was it the kid I saw? Was he down in the cellar?

I left the pantry and entered the living room in time to collide with Brad.

"What happened?" he asked.

"I think there is someone else here," I said. "I saw a kid earlier, and I think he's in the cellar."

"Mort said he didn't have a kid."

"And you suddenly trust Mort now?" I demanded.

I moved past him to leave the cabin. He followed me outside, down the steps, and around to the chained doors leading to the cellar under the cabin.

"The cellar is locked," Brad said. "How could the kid have gotten in the cellar and locked it from the outside?"

"I know what I saw," I snapped.

Brad backed away, holding his hands up.

"I'm not saying I doubt what you saw. But …"

"I'm not going crazy!" I yelled. "There's something in the damn cellar."

I stomped on the flat wooden doors, as if that would force them open.

"What do you want me to do? Cut the chains?"

"Fuck it," I growled, turning away from Brad and hurrying around the side of the cabin, back up the stairs.

"Hey," he called, following me. "I didn't mean to piss you off."

"Did you get the radio working?" I demanded angrily.

"Yeah," he said, averting my eyes. "I think so. But there wasn't a response. I'll keep trying." He turned and went back down the hallway.

I almost followed him, but stopped. I didn't want to be around him. I returned to the kitchen to clean up the mess I had made. Once I wiped up the pile of mush and scrubbed the floor, I sat on the couch in the living room. It was surprisingly comfortable, despite the thin cushions.

This was a cute and cozy cabin.

I couldn't imagine living there for half a year, but it would be a nice quiet place to retreat to from time to time. The couch sat directly in front of the fireplace. Small framed pictures sat on the rail above it. I stood up to look at them.

There was one of a younger burly man with wiry dark hair who I assumed was Mort. Another picture was of him and a woman who must have been his wife. She was a gorgeous Native American woman, with long black hair down to her waist. They both looked so happy, standing in the meadow outside. My eyes came to a third picture. After staring at it for several seconds, I picked it up in my hands.

"He lied," I called aloud.

The photo was of Mort, his wife, and a dark-haired boy I was positive was the same boy I saw earlier. "Why would he lie?" I grasped the photo and hurried to the back room to find Brad.

He was sitting at a narrow desk in front of an old, antique-looking radio. It was the only other piece of furniture in the room besides a bed.

"I think I got through," he said, his tone excited. "I heard a voice, and I think he heard me. I think help might actually be coming."

"Mort lied," I said, not sharing his enthusiasm. I slammed the photo down on the desk in front of him. "There is a boy, and he's here somewhere around here."

Brad didn't say anything. He stared at the picture for a long while.

"Are you sure this is the boy you saw?"

"Yes." I said.

Brad turned to me, his eyes revealing his worry.

"Case, this picture looks old. Look at Mort; he's got to be at least ten years younger in this picture. And that boy, well … he wouldn't be a boy anymore."

I sighed and almost collapsed in frustration.

"I know that," I said weakly. "I fucking know that."

I felt like I'd lost it completely. I covered my face in my hands, so I wouldn't have to look Brad in the face. Brad didn't say anything. I felt his weight beside me on the bed, felt his arm slide around me as he pulled me close to him.

"Brad, this is going to sound ridiculous. I know it's impossible. But I don't think Mort knows he's dead."

"His son?"

"No," I said, pulling away from Brad. "The dead man in the woods, the one hanging from the tree." I remembered the dead body swaying in my mind. "That was Mort. And the woman, that was his wife."

Brad stood up and backed away as if he was suddenly afraid of me.

"Don't look at me like that," I said. "I know it sounds impossible, but … I think the whole family is dead. I think their spirits are trapped here."

"I think this whole murderer thing has gotten to you," he said softly. "Which is totally understandable. We've gone through a lot so fast. It's gotten to me, too. But it's okay, Case. We'll get out of here, and things will get back to normal."

I looked up at him, staring down at me sympathetically. It infuriated me. Why couldn't he understand?

"I think this is the spare room. We can sleep here. I'll go make us something to eat. You just relax."

I didn't say anything. I just watched him walk away as he escaped the room.

Mort had been gone a while. I wondered when he'd return—or if he'd return at all. I spread out across the bed and looked up at the ceiling. I'm not crazy. My eyes burned into the wood. I tried my hardest to shut my brain down, and to focus solely on what was physically in front of me. I kept staring at the ceiling. It didn't work. I don't think I blinked for an hour. I just listened to the noises of whatever it was moving around in the cellar below me. I didn't move until Brad returned to the room with two bowls of rice and beans. I sat up, and he handed one to me. We both ate in silence. I spoke first after I had eaten everything.

"I don't want to wait for help. I just want to get out of here. Can we please just go?"

"In the morning, we'll go." He took the bowl from me, but didn't move off the bed. "We just have to make it another day or so—that's all."

He stood up and took the bowls out of the room. I watched as he walked down the hall. I was about to lay back down flat on the bed, but a sound across the room made me jump. Something thumped against the floor. I looked over at the desk chair. Brad's red jacket was draped over its back. A small black box sat on the floor below the chair. I got up and knelt down to pick it up. This must be what Brad was looking so hard for at the campsite.

I opened the box to find a shiny gold band with a single small diamond in the center. I inhaled loudly. My brain was flooded with so many thoughts I couldn't focus on a single one. I felt arms slide around my waist from behind.

When did Brad reenter the room?

I felt him kiss the back of my neck.

"If we make it through this together …" I began, "If we make it home, I promise I'll forgive you."

"I love you," he said and kissed the top of my head.

I turned around, and Brad took the box from my hand and took out the ring. I smiled when he placed the ring on my finger.

"I just want to be with you," he said. "Stay with me, and I'll always protect you. Will you be mine forever? And if you are mine, you have to know that I'm also yours."

I reached out and grabbed the back of his neck and pressed my lips against his. He was surprised, but he didn't resist. I closed my eyes and felt his tongue entangle with mine. We fell on the bed, and I felt his weight suddenly on top of me. I held him as tightly as our bodies would allow.

"I promise," I whispered in his ear. "Get us home, and I'll be yours."

I licked his neck and bit down hard on it. He moaned, and suddenly he was pinning me down and ravishing my face with kisses. I closed my eyes as our lips touched again. I felt wetness drip down on my cheeks. I opened my eyes and screamed.

I didn't dare explain to him what I had seen in place of his face—instead I shoved him away, and then I was up off the bed and fleeing the room. I was hysterical, and as I ran down the hallway … I ran right into Brad, who entered the hallway from the kitchen.

"Case …" he called my name, his tone worried. "What's wrong?"

I couldn't speak. I was as confused as I was terrified and I couldn't utter a legitimate word. I looked back to the bedroom, the door ajar. The bed was empty.

Brad had been in the room with me. But he was in the kitchen.

How could he be in two places at once? It wasn't possible.

Brad's eyes suddenly turned from worried to angry, and his grip on my wrist tightened. He lifted up my hand to his face and his eyes narrowed as he focused on the ring on my finger.

"You went through my things?"

"It fell on the floor, and you … you were in the room, but then it wasn't you, and …"

My voice was strident, on the verge of hysteria, and I lost all words. I turned back to the doorway of the room again; the bed was still empty. I know I sounded like a lunatic; I probably looked it, too.

"Case, I …"

"I'm not crazy!" I yelled, and yanked my hand away from him. I turned and ran across the living room toward the front door.

"Case," he called loudly behind me.

Outside, the sky was darkening, and the night's first stars were opening their bright eyes. I jumped off the porch and ran around the side of the cabin, toward the cellar doors.

"Case …" I heard Brad's voice from inside the house once again.

"I'm not crazy," I said aloud, in a pathetic attempt to convince myself that I wasn't actually losing it. "I'm not fucking crazy."

I stared down at the cellar doors as if they were going to open for me. I moved past them and around the side of the house. There stood a tall rectangular shed, and there was no lock hanging on the door. I opened the shed door and immediately found an axe with a bright yellow handle resting against the wall closest to me. It felt heavy in my hands as I lifted it. I carried the axe back to the cellar doors and raised the blade over my head.

"I'll prove it," I said aloud to no one. I brought my hands down, but they suddenly felt light.

"What the hell do you think you're doing?" Brad demanded, appearing beside me. He lifted the axe in front of him and stared at me like I was insane.

"I'm going to prove I'm not crazy," I said. "There's something in the cellar. I know it."

"Well, instead of bashing it open like a nutcase, why not just use the key?" He sounded so angry.

I turned my head toward him, but didn't move. I watched his facial expression change from furious to sympathetic.

"You were holding it all wrong, anyway," he joked. "You'd never cut through the chain."

"Where would we find the key?" I asked through gritted teeth.

"You didn't notice the keys hanging by the door, did you?" he asked. "I noticed them after you dragged me out here earlier."

He turned around and headed back to the front door, carrying the axe with him.

"One of them is probably the cellar key."

I didn't follow him. I stood there and waited until he returned, carrying the keys. He wasn't holding the axe.

"Now I'm going to show you that there is nothing to be afraid of, okay?" Brad said. He offered me a gentle smile.

I said nothing and crossed my arms over my chest. I suddenly didn't want to go down there at all, but I couldn't turn back after making this big scene. He knelt down and fiddled with the lock.

"It's got to be this small one," he said aloud to himself.

Sure enough, the lock opened. He tugged the lock off the chain and pulled the metal links from the door handles. He glanced back at me, but didn't say anything. He pulled the doors open.

A narrow staircase led to the darkness below the cabin. Brad looked back at me again. His eyes gleamed in the moonlight, and there, there was that twisted smile, the same one from my dream.

"Maybe we shouldn't," I said weakly.

"You were just so determined that you were going to chop open the doors; now you don't want to go?" He was already making his way down.

Why didn't he grab a flashlight?

"I was … you know, emotional and having a fit. I'm relaxed now."

It was too late. He had already disappeared into the darkness, and I might as well have been talking to myself. I peered down and couldn't see anything.

"Oh man, you've got to see this." I heard him call.

How was he able to see anything at all?

"Hurry up."

I took a cautious step into the opening and onto the top step. The darkness below seemed busy somehow, as if things were moving everywhere.

"Casey," I heard Brad's voice. "Casey, I can't find the keys."

His voice wasn't coming from down in the cellar; it was coming from the other side of the house. My entire body was shaking in panic and terror. I turned to flee from the doorway, but as I turned, I came face-to-face with black eyes and greenish-gray skin.

It was Mort's dead face. Mort shoved me, and I fell backward into the cellar and tumbled down the hard, wooden steps into total darkness.

I heard the cellar doors slam shut. My head hit the ground, hard. Everything was fuzzy and I was seeing stars. I groaned. My head was spinning, and I struggled to move. I blinked the stars from my eyes, and as the floating dots faded, my fear rose to the surface as I realized that I was both totally vulnerable and not alone.

Whoever—or whatever—I had followed down here, it sure as hell wasn't Brad. I saw two small lights in the distance, a candle flame, perhaps. I could hear the whispering all around me. I sat up and moved my legs around. Nothing was broken. I peered into the darkness—shadows seemed to be moving everywhere, but I didn't see a single person.

"Casey?" I heard Brad shout from outside. My eyes went up to the closed doors of the cellar.

I opened my mouth to say something, but my voice cut off when I felt hot breath on my neck, and heard something growl, lowly and dangerously, in my ear.

I cried out and rolled over to attempt to escape, but something grabbed my leg. I couldn't see its face, but I knew what it looked like from my dream. His grip on my leg tightened, and I felt a sharp pain, like knives cutting through my flesh.

I thought I was screaming. My mouth was open, but no sound escaped me. There was no sound at all, save the sound of my body being dragged across the ground. I grabbed and clawed at the ground, trying to grip anything at all. My hand grasped something in the dirt, but the object ripped free. It was hard and rough. I held onto it. Maybe I could use it as a weapon.

The thing dragged me to the far wall and stopped. I could make out the flickering lights above on what must have been a table or shelf. The thing stood over the lights. It growled again, but not at me. It let go of my leg, and I clutched it to me. I knew my shin was bleeding. I scooted away from him, and clutched the blunt object to my chest.

I blinked, and he was gone, his shadow no longer blocking the candlelight. I scanned the entire cellar but saw nothing but darkness. I struggled to my feet. My leg burned like hell, but I could walk fine. I looked down at the table, and I realized the two lights were from a single candle. A candle was burning inside of a skull, and the lights shone through the eye sockets. The skull looked similar to a human being's, but it wasn't human. It was too big, and the teeth were abnormally long and sharp.

There were strange symbols drawn onto the wood of the table, including the one I had seen on the bodies—the moon and skull. I set the object down on the table beside the skull, and I realized it was a human bone, probably from someone's arm. I looked behind me into the dark. Someone died down here.

I turned back to the skull with the flame in its eyes. I stared at it for a long time. I found myself literally unable to look away. I stood there, entranced, for a long time. The light seemed to spread, and I was suddenly aware of red, glimmering markings all over the walls. The skull itself seemed to take on a light of its own, glowing an angry red. I slowly reached out to it, as if my arm was moving on its own. My fingers touched the hot bone, and I was swallowed in its fury as everything in my head became red, and then finally black.

When I came to, I found myself outside in the night. Once again, I was standing over the dead body of the man with the crushed skull. The air was foggy around me, and my sight blurred and refocused. Seconds later, I was in the campsite where Brad and I discovered the two bodies.

I heard the familiar scream of the woman, Mort's Native American wife. I saw her half-running, half-dragging herself across the clearing toward the trees. Her left leg had been slashed by something. I lifted my hands, but didn't see my hands—instead they were replaced by long, skinny, pale-brown fingers, and razor-sharp nails. I moved across the campsite with alarming speed and tackled the woman to the ground.

She let out another ear-piercing shriek as we both went down. I tore into her. I felt her flesh fall apart beneath my fingernails. A second later I was her, feeling everything, the weight of the creature pinning me down, the hot sting of each cut as its nails pierced my body. I looked up into its disfigured face, wide mouth, its teeth, its black eyes with red irises. I was the creature, and I was its victim, all at the same time, experiencing both the terror and the thrill, the immense pain and sadistic pleasure.

Suddenly I was somewhere else, watching in the shadows from behind a tree. Mort stood over his wife with a small blade in his hand. The woman's dead eyes stared blankly up at Mort. He was weeping. He used her blood to draw the symbol on her arm. A moment later, I saw Mort across the campsite. He was hanging from the tree, swaying back and forth, his body twitching until all life left him. I scanned the campsite, basking in my masterpiece. I saw eyes behind every tree staring back at me. So many eyes. So many dead.

Seconds later, I was standing on the porch of the cabin, looking out at a field of gray corpses instead of purple flowers. I poked my head around the corner of the building, staring at the long-haired boy. I jumped over the railing to the ground below, and ran after him.

"Who are you?" I cried out.

He looked at me and smiled, his eyes gleaming in the sunlight. He turned to run, disappearing behind the back the cabin. I ran after him.

"Wait," I called.

I hurried down the side of the cabin until I reached the corner. When I turned, something hit my chest hard, clotheslining me. I dropped to the ground, and all of the air escaped my lungs. I coughed and gasped for breath. I looked up at Brad, stared into his eyes, his angry eyes.

"He's going to kill you," someone whispered into my ear. A child's voice.

I looked over and saw the boy lying beside me, his head beside mine, his black eyes locked with mine. The boy's skin was gray and rotting, and the all-too-familiar death smell slithered up my nostrils. I knew those were his bones down in the cellar.

He grabbed my wrist, and immediately I was pulled into his vision. I saw him opening the cellar door and climbing into the darkness. The doors locked behind him, chained shut. Mort stood over the chained doors, his head hung low. He was sobbing. The doors were being pushed up, but to no avail. The chains sealed the boy inside.

"I told you never to go down there. You have to fight it," Mort said to the screaming child below. "Only you can fight it now."

The boy let go of my hand, and I was once again beside him on the ground.

"Daddy," he said, his voice menacing.

He grabbed my hand again, and I saw Mort standing over the cellar doors once more. His hair was different, longer and graying.

"You stop it, you bastard!" he called down to whatever was pushing up against the doors. "You aren't my son. My son is dead." He sobbed.

"Daddy, please!" it called from below. "I miss you so much. Let me out."

Mort's sobs turned to anger as he ripped at the chains, unlatched the lock with his key, and flung open the doors, as if he was ready to fight whatever was calling to him. He stormed into the darkness below, cursing the whole way. The boy let my wrist go again, and I lay in the dirt beside him.

I looked back up at Brad. Meredith was standing next to him, smiling down at me. Her hand rested on Brad's shoulder. Brad held the yellow ax in his hands. He raised it above his head, but the sharp end was facing away from me. He brought the heavy, blunt end down on my face.

A moment later, I was screaming, and Brad was hovering over me. I brought my closed fist up to his face and struck him. My knuckles connected to his jaw. He winced in pain, and I rolled away from him. My head hurt worse than it did before, but I realized I was still in the cellar. I scrambled to my feet and dove for the stairs.

"What the fuck is wrong with you?" Brad grabbed me from behind and tugged me back.

The struggle caused him to drop whatever light he was holding. I flailed and kicked, my foot sending the light rolling away. The bright glow focused on the table, and as I fought back, I noticed the skull was gone.

"Stay the hell away from me!" I screamed, trying to pull away, punching backward and failing miserably.

"Casey, stop it!" He got his arms around mine and squeezed. I kicked backward and hit his shin with the back of my boot.

"Damn it!" He tossed me aside, and I hit the ground hard. "Case, you're fucking losing it. Stop attacking me."

"I won't let you kill me!" I shouted. I ran for the stairs.

"Casey, you know I'd never hurt you."

I didn't stop. I was up the stairs and breathed in a breath of the fresh night air. I ran through the field of flowers toward the trees.

"Case, stop!" Brad yelled.

He must have been running after me. I looked back and saw him right behind me. I didn't stop; I kept running. In desperation, I picked up speed. I saw movement all around the edge of the forest, as if things were walking in between the trees and disappearing behind them. My speed slowed, as I was suddenly just as afraid of what was ahead of me. Brad tackled me from behind and we dropped to the ground. His weight pinned me down.

"Get off me!"

"Casey, I'm not going to hurt you. You have to know that. You have to fucking know that."

He was so much stronger than me. I couldn't get up; I couldn't move. I felt him lying down on top of me, forcing my arms and legs down.

"I don't know what happened to you down there, I don't know what's going on around here but … I believe you now." His voice was right in my ear.

I stopped moving. I was breathing so fast and heavily. He kissed the side of my head.

"I believe you." He kissed my head again. "Please just, don't leave me. I need you, Case, but I need you to keep it together if we are going to make it out of here. I need you to relax. I promise you I'm not going to hurt you; I'd never in a million years hurt you."

You already did, I thought. I took in a deep breath and tried to force myself to relax.

"Why do you believe me now?"

Brad's weight left me as he rose to his knees, and he sat down beside me. I pushed myself up off the ground to my knees and met his gaze.

He honestly looked frightened.

Was he scared of me?

"Case, how did you get inside that cellar?"

"I …" I couldn't bring myself to say it, but I believe the fear on my face was greater than his, and he noticed.

I think I actually started to cry. I felt warm wetness slide down my face. He placed his hand on the back of my head and pulled it toward his. He touched his forehead to mine.

"I was so worried when I couldn't find you. The damn cellar, it was still locked from the outside."

"It trapped me down there, and it …" My words stopped as I tried to process the visions I had seen. "It's like it crawled into my head and showed me things. Terrible things. I think I'm starting to understand it."

"What are you talking about?" He pulled away and forced me to look at him again.

I didn't say anything else. I was afraid that speaking about the thing would make it real—but it was already real. I had been touched by the devil, enveloped by his darkness, felt the glory of pain, and I could only imagine what that meant.

"We are getting out of here now," he said.

"No," I said softly. "We can't leave tonight."

"Why the hell not? You don't really want to stay here, do you?"

"No, but we can't go out there now, either. Not with them all around us."

"Case, you're scaring me."

"I know," I said. "Trust me, I know. But they seem less active during the day. And I haven't seen the … whatever it is, during the day. I've only seen it at night. I thought he was just a psycho in the woods, but he's not, Brad. He's so much worse than that."

Brad looked away from me toward the trees. I'm not sure if he even heard me. He probably still thought I was crazy. But then his face changed, and his eyes went wide with horror. He jumped up and pulled me to my feet.

"Back inside right now," he said, and we were moving, sprinting back toward the cabin.

I'm not sure what he saw, but I certainly wasn't going to argue. That cabin in the woods terrified me, but the woods terrified me more. We were up the stairs and inside the cabin, and Brad slammed and locked the door behind us. A lantern rested on a mantle above the fireplace. Brad leaned back against the door, as if he expected someone to break it down.

"What did you see?" I asked, out of breath. I grabbed the lantern from the fireplace. Brad didn't have time to answer.

There was a loud crash against the door. Brad was so startled he took a step back before pressing his shoulder against the door. He pulled out his pistol. I had never felt such fear, but I rushed beside Brad and pressed my back against the door, forcing all of my weight against it. There wasn't a second crash. Instead there was a long scratching noise, as if someone was dragging a blade against the wood outside. The scratching noise slowly moved away from the door, to the only window in the room in between the door and the fireplace. It paused, probably peeking through the glass. Then the scratching moved farther away.

When it reached the edge of the porch, it turned around and slowly drew closer until it was standing just outside the door again. We listened for what felt like minutes before we heard a voice on the other end.

"Hey, Brad. Casey? Let me in." There was a knock on the door. It was Mort's voice.

Brad moved his hand toward the doorknob.

"Don't open the door," I whispered while grabbing the front of his jacket. "It's not Mort; Mort is dead. Don't open the door."

"I don't have my key, guys," Mort's voice came through the door again. "Open up. I found my wife; she's hurt real bad." His voice was desperate now. "Please help us. There's so much blood."

Brad stared at me, searching my eyes for truth or reason.

"It can make itself look like anyone," I explained.

Brad looked torn and confused. He moved to the side of the door, by the window, and peered outside.

"Oh my God," he said.

He moved to the door. I jumped in front of him.

"Don't!" I shouted.

"Stop it, Casey," he said, shoving me out of the way.

I caught a glimpse of what was outside in the darkness. I froze. I stared through the window. Mort stood outside. He held a lantern, and his wife, the exact woman from my dream. Her arm dangled loosely down to the ground. She wasn't moving. She was blood-soaked. So was he. Brad unlocked the door and opened it.

We both screamed together this time.

In the half-second it took for the door to open, Mort, his wife, and the light of the lantern were gone. Instead, the ungodly horror from my dreams stood in the doorway, its red pupils aglow. Its thin, rubbery lips curved up in a smile, showing off its sharp teeth. It raised its long skinny arms and outstretched its claws.

Brad jumped backward, aimed his gun, and pulled the trigger. He fired three times in rapid succession. All three bullets hit.

The creature howled in rage and exploded in a cloud of black smoke. Its cries didn't vanish, however; the sound only grew louder. The smoke swirled around in the doorway. The lantern in my hands went out. Brad slammed the door shut and locked it.

The rage cry grew louder, so loud that I dropped the dead lantern on the floor and brought my hands up to cover my ears. I felt the floorboards beneath my feet being pushed upward. I staggered backward, and I saw Brad stumble as well. Even in the dark, I could see the deeper darkness oozing its way through the cracks around the door.

"Let's move!" Brad shouted to me.

We both sprinted toward the back of the cabin, but a floorboard lifted just high enough to clip the bottom of my boot, and I stumbled and fell to my knees. I looked up and saw Brad turn the corner down the hall toward the back rooms.

Wait, no, he was moving into the kitchen …

He disappeared around the corner.

"Casey!" I heard Brad's worried shout.

Even his voice seemed to be coming from two places. I looked behind me and immediately noticed the black smoke was gone. Instead, it was waiting for me to choose the wrong direction. I stood up and decided to run down the hallway to the back room. Brad stood there in the doorway, waiting for me. In the darkness, I could see the relief on his face. He reached out his hand and grasped mine.

"Casey, wait …" I heard a voice behind me. I turned and saw Brad standing at the far end of the hall.

"Where are you going?"

I turned to the Brad in front of me. He yanked my arm so hard that I stumbled forward into the room and onto the bed.

"Casey, no!" The Brad standing in the hallway cried and ran at full speed toward us. The Brad in the bedroom slammed the door shut and braced himself against it.

"What the fuck is happening?" the Brad in the room with me asked.

There was a slam against the outside of the door.

"I don't understand."
I stared at him, unable to speak.

Who was I in the room with? My boyfriend—or the devil himself?

There were repeated slams against the door, but the Brad in the room with me managed to keep it shut. It was toying with me. It could have killed me. It had multiple opportunities to shred my flesh with its claws.

"On the table ..." He sounded out of breath. "There's a map I found." The crashing against the door suddenly stopped. "There's a road. It can't be more than six or seven miles north from here. We can make it there tonight."

"Why didn't you tell me this earlier?" I managed to choke out, unable to hide the suspicion and fear in my voice.

"I found it while you were missing," he said, his back still against the door.

I wondered where the second Brad had wandered off to.

"Why are you looking at me like that?" There was worry in his voice.

I moved to the desk and picked up the map. It was too dark for me to really study it, not that it would have mattered. I'm directionally challenged and would probably have headed east if Brad weren't there to guide me. I folded the map and put it in my pocket. I'd worry about it later, if we somehow escaped certain death.

Why was I still alive?

"We're trapped," I said. "How are we going to get out of here?"

As if in response to my question, there was an explosion of glass and wood as the only window in the room shattered inward and a wooden chair crashed onto the floor.

"Case, hurry!" Brad shouted to me from outside.

I didn't hesitate. I grabbed my backpack off the floor and charged to the window, glass crunching beneath my boots.

"No!" the Brad standing inside the room screamed. "Casey, he'll kill you!"

I quite literally dove headfirst out the broken window and into Brad's arms. He set me on the ground, grasped my hand, and we sprinted into the meadow.

"We have to go north," I sputtered, out of breath, yet I didn't allow myself to slow down.

"There's a road that way. We can get out of here."

Brad didn't say anything, but he altered our course and pulled me along in a direction I could only hope was north. He pulled a flashlight out of his pocket and shone the light ahead. From behind me, the Brad inside the house repeatedly shouted my name. He was pleading for me to stop, warning me of the creature I was running with.

The decision had been easy. I was simply trading one devil for another. This devil just happened to be outside, which was closer to my goal of escaping. If it happened to be the real Brad, great. If it wasn't, I was still getting the hell out of there.

I looked back and didn't see anyone chasing after us, but that didn't mean he wasn't there. The meadow looked so different this time. The light from the flashlight revealed the flowers ahead, only they weren't violet and welcoming anymore. Instead, they looked menacing, as their petals and their leaves were black and shriveled.

Brad abruptly stopped, and I accidentally rammed him in the back. The flowers ahead were definitely moving. A mound of earth rose up, and something long dead slithered up from the ground and stood. Flowers were stuck to the corpse, as their roots were embedded into its greenish flesh. Brad and I screamed together, and the flashlight he was holding flickered and went out .Darkness consumed us.

We heard a low moan ahead from the creature, and then a second moan behind us. I pulled off my backpack to fish for my flashlight, but Brad was suddenly tugging me to the right. I followed him, dragging my backpack with my free hand. I couldn't see where we were going, and I didn't know which was more terrifying: not knowing what might be lurking ahead, or knowing what was lurking ahead.

My eyes were quickly adjusting to the surrounding darkness, and I saw shadows moving everywhere.

The field of corpses from my vision, they were rising all around us as trapped souls crawled back into their bodies. They didn't want us to leave, that much I knew, although I'm not sure how I knew it. There was something buried in my brain now, a fragmented curse of a dark knowledge that I couldn't quite process.

"Something's changed," I said to Brad. "The forest, it's never been like this before."

"We can make it," he said, his voice determined. "I'm not going to let you die here."

I knew he must have been terrified, but the strength behind his words made me believe him, made me believe that I had chosen right.

We were quickly approaching the trees, and another rotting thing reached up from the earth. No time to stop, no time to change direction. Without a word, we both jumped over it. Our boots cleared its bony fingers, but it grasped my dangling backpack. The tug was enough to stop me in my tracks. Brad didn't let go of my other hand, and I found myself pulled in two directions at once. I didn't let go of the bag. I kept tugging. Brad pulled out his gun and shot the corpse in its face. Flesh and bone splattered from it. Black ooze dripped from its eye socket. It let go of my bag, but it didn't stop moving. It continued its climb from the earth, moving faster now with fury behind its movements.

I looked behind the creature at all the dead things erupting from the earth, and my jaw dropped to the dirt. This meadow was a burial ground. Maybe this entire area of the forest was a burial ground. I couldn't fathom why Mort and his wife had chosen this place to live, but I knew that they knew their cabin was built on top of the dead, with that thing in the cellar.

Maybe this was my fault. Maybe I made it worse. I should have never gone down there.

"Come on," Brad said loudly, bringing me back to reality.

We turned and ran into the trees. The creatures ran after us. Brad shot at the two closest to us, but the shots only slowed them down. The gun was useless. These things were already dead; they couldn't die again. They would pursue us tirelessly until they caught us, and they would drag us down with them into death. Brad dropped his empty gun on the ground, and we continued to run.

Even without light, Brad quickly navigated us through the trees. We zigzagged between tree trunks and ducked below twisted branches. Desperation pumped adrenaline through my veins, and we ran without slowing down for what felt like forever. We couldn't stop. To stop was to die and be stuck there forever. I didn't want this to be my eternal resting place. The moans were getting softer, and less frequent.

Were we actually outrunning them?

Maybe their decayed legs were slower than ours.

"We're gonna make it," Brad said to me.

We jogged for almost an hour before we slowed down

and stopped. I wasn't able to run anymore, but I quickly realized that it would have been better to keep going. As adrenaline left me, so did my strength, and with fatigue came nausea. I coughed until I knelt over and vomited. Brad rubbed my back as I did.

"It's okay, baby, just let it out. I think we put some distance between us and them."

"How much farther?" I asked.

"A couple miles," he said. "But we can make it."

"I don't know how much longer I can keep this up," I said.

I leaned back against a skinny tree. I looked around us at the surrounding area, and then my attention turned to the moon. An eerie and uncomfortable feeling slithered over me. The moon was full again, and this small clearing we stood in, it looked familiar. It was familiar.

We had been there before—twice before.

Brad didn't seem to notice. He was focused entirely on me. He had no idea that somehow, we'd run in a complete circle. It wasn't possible; none of this was possible. But it had happened.

"So, I noticed you haven't taken the ring off yet," he said to me. He had almost caught his breath.

Was he trying to distract me? Get me to focus on something other than fatigue and fear?

I looked down at my hand. The gold band. I'd forgotten about it.

Why was he bringing this up to me now? Didn't he know that we were never getting out of here? We were as good as dead.

"I know this isn't the time, but …" He stepped up to me and knelt down in front of me and grabbed my hand. "I don't know if there will be another time, but if I'm going to die, I want you to know how much I love you, and how much I hate myself for hurting you."

I looked around the small clearing. The five stones were surrounding us. The wind picked up and I heard the rush of whispers.

"Brad, I …"

"Let me finish," he said. "I …" He didn't get to finish his words. Something knocked into both of us, and we both crumbled to the ground.

I rolled away as Brad struggled to get up. I realized that Brad was fighting with Brad. They rolled over on top of each other in the dirt and leaves, wrestling, and striking at each other's faces with their fists.

"Run!" the Brad on the ground yelled.

The Brad on top of him had one hand around his throat while the one on the ground tried to prevent him from punching him with his other fist. I didn't run. Instead I ran up to them and kicked the Brad on top in the head. I pulled the knife from my belt and held it up. The Brad I'd kicked rolled over off him and cried out in pain. The other Brad struggled to get up.

"What the hell?" the Brad I had kicked yelled. "Case, it's me."

"No, Casey," the other Brad said. He was on his

knees now, gasping for breath. "It's me. You have to know it's me."

I brought both of my fists up to my head in frustration. I didn't know what to do. I backed away from them both, and pointed the knife at each of them.

"Casey …" the Brad I had kicked called out. "I love you. Please, you have to trust me."

"Case …" the other Brad called. "You know I'd never hurt you. Never. I'd die for you."

It was toying with me, why was it toying with me? What was the point of the charade when it could just kill us both and be done with it?

And then it hit me, all at once, in a rush as the fragmented knowledge wove together into a tapestry of horrors inside my brain. Mort's words, the corpses, the boy in the cellar, the repeated full moon, the skull, this place we were standing in for the third time. That thing—it needed me. It never hurt me, despite ample opportunity to do so, especially when I was alone with it. It didn't want to hurt me. It needed me. It just wanted to escape this woodland prison, same as us. It can take the form of any one of its victims. That's what Mort had said. I was never his victim.

It was Brad. It had always been Brad. That body, that first crime scene: that was the beginning, and that was also the end. It needed me. It wanted to leave, and it could only leave with me. It needed me, and if it needed me, then that meant that I could fight it. Both of them were on their feet now, but neither Brad moved.

"Casey, get out of here," the Brad on the left said. "Just run."

"I can't leave," I said. "Not yet. None of us can. That's what this is all about, right?"

I wasn't sure where the strength in my voice came from. Desperation, maybe? I was certainly at my breaking point.

"What do you mean?" the Brad on the left asked.

"I can get us home, babe," I said to no one in particular.

Don't worry. He ain't gonna kill ya. Mort's words repeated in my head. I recalled the album of visions the thing had revealed to me in the cellar. I could visit each scene so clearly, as the memories were embedded in my head. It never meant to kill me. It didn't actually kill anyone. It drove others to kill instead. Mort left his son to die in that cellar, and then it continued to tempt Mort with his son's voice until he couldn't resist, and he, too, went down into that hell.

It drove Mort to kill his wife. Then, instead of freeing the demon, Mort hung himself. It relished in the death it caused and lived the violence vicariously through its tormented targets, that much I had felt for myself, and yet, Mort had said that it wanted to be free.

The chained cellar, those symbols on the walls, that place was meant to entomb him, and I let him lure me down there, just as it did that boy. I wondered if Mort was ever really with us at all, if it was actually his spirit or just the demon parading around as him.

I guess it didn't matter. Either way, Mort or the devil, he told me exactly what he wanted. He led us right where he wanted. I was the key to his freedom. What freedom meant to a demon, I could only guess. It probably wanted to be free to wreak havoc upon the world.

"I can free us, Brad. I just have to kill the right one."

Both Brads looked at each other, then at me.

"Casey, you can tell who I am, right?" the Brad on the right said. "You've known me since we were dumb kids. You know me better than anyone. You're the only person who has ever really known me and loved me."

"Shut up!" the other Brad yelled. "Nice try, but Case knows me. We are bonded. We've been to hell and back. I'm so sorry that I ever hurt you. You are the best thing that has ever happened to me, and I will never hurt you again. I can't live without you." He stepped forward. "You have to trust me."

Trust, trust, trust, who could I trust?

I heard low moans in the distance. I turned away from them for a second to look back. The dead weren't far behind. They'd be coming for us. I was running out of time.

"Get away from him!" Brad yelled, moving forward and shoving the one standing in front of me out of the way. "I know I ruined things, Casey, and I know that all my life I've screwed things up and you have been there to fix it. Things were going so well, and then I …"

"Don't say it," I said, clenching my fists. "I don't want to think about it."

"We've been avoiding it for so long, Casey," he said, walking closer to me.

"Stay back!" I screamed.

He didn't. He stepped right up to me, and tried to pull me in with his dual eyes.

"I'm sorry. I'm so sorry."

I stared into his lovely, stupid eyes.

"Please don't say it," I pleaded, my voice weak and wet.

"Meredith and I, we——"

I stabbed him.

He didn't cry out, didn't scream, just inhaled deeply and staggered back. I stabbed him again and dragged the knife down his chest.

"Why?" was all he could mutter.

His eyes were so hurt, betrayed, and fearful, even loving. His eyes loved me, despite me killing him.

"Casey, you did it," my boyfriend said.

The Brad I had stabbed fell back onto the ground, and I dropped to my knees and cut him again, and again. Without thinking, I picked up one of the nearby rocks, and bashed it over his black eye. I bashed his head again and again and again. I felt so much rage, but also triumph. I'd won, and we would be free.

"Casey, stop." I heard his voice behind me. He grabbed my wrist, and the rock fell from my hand to the earth.

"That's enough." He lifted me up and held me.

The moans were louder now; the creatures were almost to us. I pulled away from Brad and dropped to my knees beside the body.

"What are you doing?"

I didn't answer. I tore away his shirt, and dipped my finger into his blood. I drew the symbol of the skull and the moon on his arm. I did my best to mimic the symbols I'd seen. That first body we found, I'm not sure how I knew it, but I had to recreate the scene exactly.

Immediately, the moans of the dead stopped. Everything quieted. I looked up at the moon, and it was no longer full. I looked down at the corpse below me, and it was gone.

"We can go now," I said.

I looked back at Brad, his eyes fixed on where the body was moments before. He looked both puzzled and relieved. He moved to me and lifted me to my feet. He kissed me.

"Oh my God, I have never loved you so much."

His arms tightened around my back, and he twirled me around.

"How did you know you could do it? How did you know it was me?"

"Because you haven't been able to say her name since it happened," I said darkly.

He nodded his head, and set me down. He didn't speak. He just looked at the ground where the corpse should have been. He laced his fingers with mine, and we walked together in silence. We hadn't walked for very long before I saw a bright light ahead. It was moving. It took me a second to realize the light was from a car's headlights.

"The road," I called. "We are almost to the road."

New energy rushed through my body, and I picked up speed. The lights were getting brighter, closer to us, but also closer to leaving us behind.

"Stop," I called. "Please stop!"

I knew my shouting was probably useless, but I didn't care. I kept running and screaming with what little breath I had. Brad was shouting along with me. I emerged from the trees and stopped when I realized there was asphalt beneath my boots. Brad ran into me, surprised by my sudden stop, and I stumbled forward, in front of the lights of the oncoming car. The car swerved, barely missed me, and came to a screeching halt, twenty feet away. I ran over to the car as the window was sliding down.

"What the hell, man?" the man behind the wheel sputtered; he seemed almost as out of breath as I was. "What are you two guys doing out here?"

"Please, sir, I need your help. We've been in the woods for days. Could you take us to the next town?

Brad closed the door of the hotel room behind us. I practically collapsed onto the bed. The sun would be up in two hours, but I planned on sleeping all day. First, I needed a shower though. I kicked off my boots and struggled to sit up. My body wanted rest, but I was determined to clean myself up. Brad stared at me for a while without saying anything. He sat down on one of the two chairs tucked under a tiny wooden table.

"What?" I asked. I sat up and moved to the edge of the bed to face him.

"I just can't believe we made it out of there. I can't believe you chose right."

I nodded my head but didn't say anything. He reached out his hand to touch mine, but I pulled away from him. I stood up and moved to the bathroom. I glanced back and saw the all-too-familiar sad and disappointed look on his face.

I stared at myself in the mirror; I had bags around my brown eyes. I looked like hell, my inch-long dark, curly hair was greasy and disheveled, and grime covered my face. I had more facial hair than I normally allowed. I never could grow a decent beard or mustache, so I preferred to be clean-shaven. I didn't have a razor, so I figured I'd have to settle for just a shower. I turned the knob on the bath and as the water heated up, I undressed. I flicked the lever and the shower sprayed overhead. I poked my head out the bathroom door and looked over at Brad. He was still by the table; he was plugging in my phone.

"Aren't you coming?" I asked with a smirk.

He lifted his head up, and his beautiful eyes met mine. His frown turned upward, and he grinned at me. He got up and hurried over to me.

After showering, I dried myself off with the towel in the main room. Brad was still in the bathroom, brushing his teeth. I sat on the edge of the bed and played with the gold ring on my finger. I did love the ring. My phone beeped. I stood up and looked at it. I had three texts from my mom and a voicemail from Meredith. I didn't feel like listening to it; instead, my stomach growled, and I realized I hadn't even stopped to think about getting food. I suddenly realized I was starving. I grabbed my backpack and opened it, hoping to find some remnant of a snack.

I dropped the bag, and my entire body shivered violently. Inside the bag was the large skull of the devil in the woods. I didn't know how it found its way there, yet at the same time, I wasn't entirely surprised it had. It was mine now. I had reached out and touched it, and I'd let it run rampant right through my subconscious. It connected with me, and as it still lingered in my head, it was still with me physically too.

Suddenly, I realized that the corpses rising from the ground were not after me. They had been after my backpack. After the skull. It wasn't supposed to leave that meadow. I wasn't supposed to leave that meadow. That's why Mort left his son to die. That's why he hung himself, not just because he was mourning his wife; he couldn't risk taking that thing out of the woods with him.

"Is something wrong?" Brad asked, standing in his towel outside the bathroom.

For half of a second, I didn't see Brad's face. I saw the creature's horrifying face, its fangs, its black and red eyes, its rubbery beige skin.

"Not at all," I said, looking over my shoulder at the table, at my phone.

When I looked back at him, he wasn't standing across the room anymore; he was hovering over me, looking down at me hungrily. He lifted my left hand up to his mouth, and kissed my ring finger, just above the gold band.

"Yes," I said.

"What?"

"Yes, I'll marry you," I said. "I keep my promises. We got out. I am yours now, and you are mine."

His eyes were thrilled. He traced my hand and wrist and arm with kisses. The truth was, when guessing which one of them was the real Brad, I realized that I couldn't trust either of them. The only thing that had really mattered was that they both needed me. Desperation was my motivation, and I was getting out of there either way, and whichever one of them was left standing would get to come along with me. Either choice would have been the right choice because either choice was freedom.

His eyes gleamed with a wicked euphoria. He traced my hand and wrist and arm with his lips.

"You know," I said, pulling him down on top of me and kissing him hard on the mouth. "I think it's time we finally give Meredith a call back."

He chuckled and lowered his mouth to kiss and nibble my neck. I buried my hand in his hair and tugged it playfully. I still wondered how it was possible that Brad had been so close to that body in the woods—he had literally knelt beside it—and yet he didn't even notice that it was his.

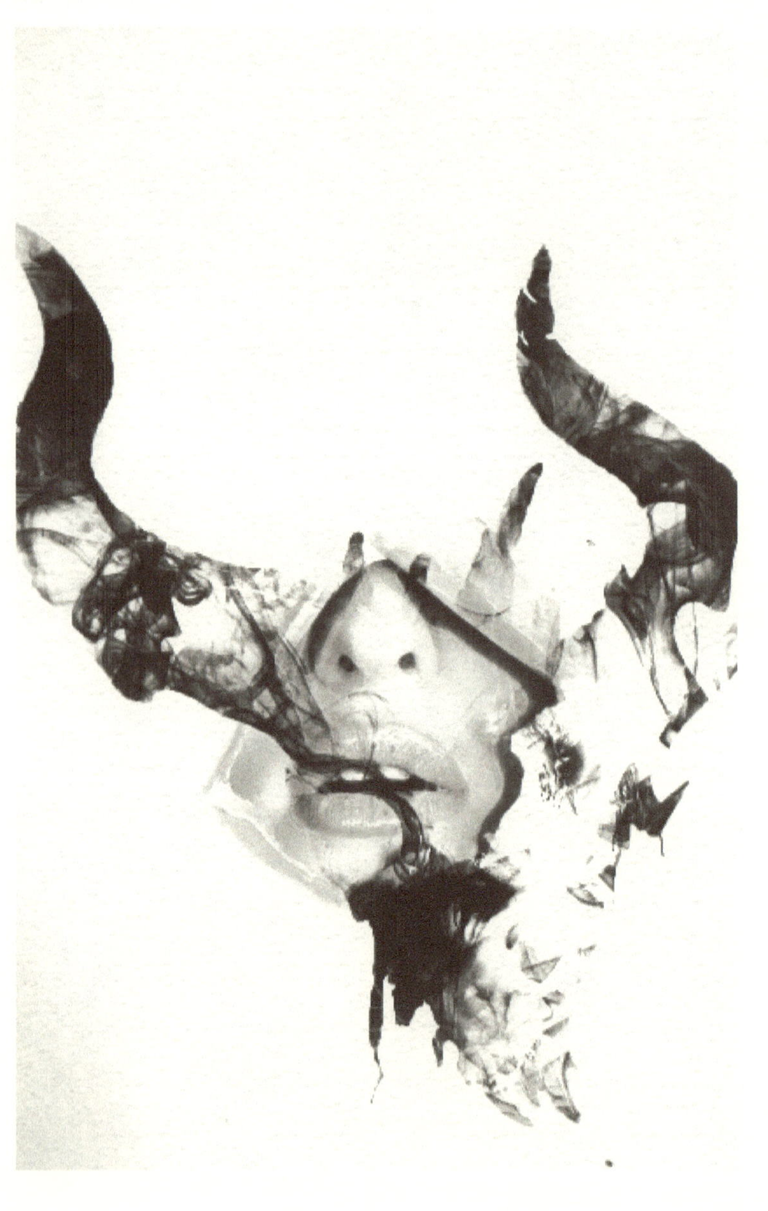

TRAUMA

When Shelly went into her daughter's room, she found the bed empty. Her blanket was half on the floor, along with the stuffed clownfish she always insisted on sleeping with.

"Justice," Shelly called. "It's time to get ready for school."

She gave the room a once-over before deciding to check downstairs. It was odd; Justice almost never woke up on her own. She loved sleeping in. As she left the room, she heard a low cough behind her. She froze, and poked her head into the room again.

"Justice?" She was greeted with silence, aside from a car starting outside.

She stepped into the room and knelt beside the bed.

"Stop playing, Justice, or you'll be late."

She poked her head under the bed, but there was nothing there except dust, shoes that were probably too small, and old, forgotten toys. She sneezed after inhaling the dust.

She groaned as she stood up. The closet. Justice hated the closet, so she wouldn't be in there. Still, Shelly realized that the blanket that was hanging off the bed trailed in the direction of the sliding glass doors of the closet.

"Justice," she called, frustrated, and moved to the doors. She forced them open, and a shrill scream blared like a fire alarm.

～ᘓᘔ～

"Where were you yesterday?" Carla asked when Shelly sat down in the small cubicle beside her.

Shelly didn't hear her, as she was too busy shuffling through her purse, searching for allergy meds. She'd been sneezing all morning, ever since inhaling the dust in her daughter's room. Shelly found a tiny bottle of water but no pills. She sighed and took a drink before sitting down at the computer.

"Hey, did you hear Elliot's getting fired?" Carla asked in her thick Jersey accent.

Shelly sneezed into the sleeve of her blouse and turned on her computer without a word. Carla's words didn't make it through the barrier of mucus that seemed to encompass Shelly's head. She reached over to her box of tissues, swiped one, and blew her nose loudly.

"Shelly, earth to Shelly. Are you sick?" Carla poked

her head over the cubicle wall.

"I'm fine," she said. "Sorry I'm late."

"It's not a big deal. Elliot's not even here, so no one can get in trouble." Her friend's voice was high with excitement. "It's casual Friday."

"It's only Thursday," Shelly reminded her.

"No, yesterday was Thursday. Today is Friday, and I have a date tonight. I made reservations at that new Greek restaurant downtown. Have you been? I'm so excited."

"No, it's Thursday," Shelly argued. "Last night was Justice's piano practice."

Her five-year-old daughter had music lessons every Wednesday. Shelly glanced up at Carla, who looked worried.

"Shelly, look at your phone."

"What for?"

"Because it's definitely Friday. Are you sure you're okay? Where were you yesterday? Were you home sick?"

"No, I wasn't home sick, I was here with you. I got written up, rememb ..."

Her voice trailed off when she saw the date on her computer screen. It was Friday.

"Okay wait, this can't be right."

"You're saying you don't remember yesterday?"

"I ... I don't know what's going on. Last night, I took Justice to her lessons, I went home, I made dinner, put her to bed and ... I drank a little wine ..."

"A little?"

"A bottle."

"Just one? That's normal, and then what?"

"And then I don't remember … I went to bed, I think."
She thought hard, but she couldn't recall a thing.

"Yeah, I watched some stupid slasher movie, and
fell asleep."

"And you slept for an entire day without remembering
a thing?"

"I couldn't have slept an entire day, not with
a kid. She …" Her voice trailed off again as she
thought about earlier.

Her ears still stung from the screaming. Justice had
obviously had one hell of a nightmare.

"She was acting a little strange this morning. She
hardly spoke to me."

She decided to leave out the part about the screaming.
She sneezed again, and then blew her nose.

"Maybe you really are sick. Maybe that's why
everything is hazy. I thought you got fed up and quit.
I was pissed, no phone call, no text; you can't just leave
a girl alone without a word. Lucky you though, Elliot
wasn't here to fire you yesterday anyway, and no one's
heard from him either. Corporate is supposed to be
sending someone out to fire him Monday. Don't ask me
how I know that."

Shelly's lips curled up into a smile.

"He's really getting canned?"

She couldn't hide the enthusiasm in her voice.

"That's the best news I've heard in a long time. I really
needed that today."

"He was the worst," Carla said. "Such an ass."

She dropped down from the cubicle wall, out of sight.

"But you should really get checked out. It's not normal to just forget a whole day, ya know?"

"I know. I really don't know what's going on with me. I'm trying to remember, but it's just a blank."

She pulled up the spreadsheet on her computer of the list of names and phone numbers she needed to call for the day.

"I really need some sales," she said out loud. "If I don't, whoever this new guy is will fire me anyway."

"Gotta get your bonus so we can go to Jamaica this summer. You need a break; your whole life's just gone down the shitter."

"Gee, thanks," Shelly grumbled.

She looked at the photo on her desk of her, Justice when she was three, and her soon-to-be-divorced wife, Macy. She wanted to cut Macy out of the photo and burn her face with a lighter.

"Can you ladies please quiet down," someone called from a nearby cubicle. "You're distracting me while I'm on the phone, and you just cost me a sale."

Shelly recognized the voice; it was Chance.

"Your shitty selling cost you the sale," Carla replied. "You're always on the bottom; why don't you try topping once in a while?"

"Carla," Shelly added, giggling.

No matter the turmoil, Carla always brightened Shelly's day. She picked up the phone to make her first call, and did her best to push the worry of having lost an entire day to the back of her mind.

After work, Shelly and Carla headed down the tan-colored hallway to the elevator. She still couldn't remember a thing from the day before. Shelly made two sales, which was satisfactory. Carla made four. Shelly didn't know what her secret was, but she guessed it was her intimidating and pushy tone. Most people couldn't say no to Carla.

"Has this happened to you before?" Carla asked. "Maybe something happened to you, and you just blocked it out. I've heard of people blocking things out that were traumatic."

"Not since I was a kid," Shelly answered honestly.

"But it did happen? When you were young?"

"I guess," she said.

"Did something happen to you?"

"I don't want to talk about it," she replied quickly. "I don't ever want to talk about my childhood. I try my best not to think about it."

"Okay then," Carla said, pressing the elevator button.

"Wait up!" they heard someone call from down the hall.

Chance fluidly flowed down the hallway, his purple shawl dancing in his wake. He was more graceful in heels than Shelly could ever be.

"Guess who made six sales today?"

"No way! That's enough for the whole week. Look at you, on top for once," Carla said.

"Don't think because I'm more of a lady than either of you hookers that I can't dominate when I want to."

The elevator doors parted, and the three of them

stepped inside. Shelly caught a glimpse of the big garnet stone around Chance's neck. It matched the small stones on his dangling earrings. She pressed the button for the parking garage. The elevator shook before starting down. Carla yelped and grasped the rail.

"Better fasten your cheek straps," Chance said, motioning to Carla's big hair. "It's a long way down."

"Yeah, I got a strap for ya," she snapped.

"Are you two getting drinks?" Chance asked.

"Shelly's sick."

"I'm not sick," Shelly said. "I'm just … I don't know what I am. But no, I'm not up for drinks today."

Her phone started vibrating in her bag. She fumbled for it and was surprised to see Macy's name on the screen. Fridays were her day to pick up Justice from school.

"Hello," she answered.

"Jesus Christ, what the hell is wrong with you?" Macy yelled into the phone.

"What do you mean?" Shelly asked, holding the device away from her ear.

"Why is our daughter scared shitless? Look, I don't care what you do with your free time, but don't just have random men over around our daughter."

"What are you talking about?"

"I'm talking about the man who left your room late last night." She snapped. "Justice said he came out of your room, and stopped in her doorway and watched her, scared the hell out of her. Keep this shit up, and you'll make me getting full custody real fucking easy."

"I didn't have anyone over last night."

"So our daughter's a liar now, then?"

"I didn't say that."

"Whatever, Shelly. Get your shit together before I take her from you for good." Macy hung up.

Shelly's hand was shaking, and she nearly dropped the phone. Her eyes watered in a whirlpool of grief and anger. By the looks on Carla and Chance's faces, they had heard every word Macy said.

"I think you really could use that drink," Chance said as the elevator doors opened.

"So, you really don't remember a thing?" Chance asked after they toasted to Shelly's shitty life. They sipped their froufrou martinis, complete with bright red cherries.

"I don't. I really don't."

"And you had a man over?" Carla asked.

"There's no way. Just the thought of inviting ANYONE into my life in a non-platonic way is enough to give me hives. I want nothing to do with dating or hooking up."

"Look, as your friend, I'm just going to come out and say it." Carla looked at Chance for reassurance. He nodded, as if he knew exactly what she was about to say.

"Maybe you were drugged," she finished.

"Drugged? Really?" she asked, her tone skeptical.

"How else would you explain the memory loss?" Chance asked. He glanced over as a male waiter in a white and brown suit walked by.

"Guys, I wasn't drugged. I don't even go out anymore, except for happy hour with you two. I just drink alone where I can make it to my own bathroom to vomit."

"You're a mess," Carla said. "Maybe you got a little drunk and decided to go out last night."

"I had my daughter all week, and I would never invite a guy over with her there. Not to mention I swore off men a long time ago."

Scrolling through her phone, she checked the previous day's activity. She had three missed calls from Carla, probably for missing work, and a text from Macy saying she would pick Justice up from school on Friday. There were no other phone calls or strange numbers added to her phone.

"Maybe she really is lying," Chance suggested. "Justice, I mean. Divorces are hard on kids. That's why I'll never have any."

"That and you're gay."

"I can still have kids, bitch; Shelly and Macy had a kid."

"You're so gay, your sperm would run from the egg."

"Guys, can we focus on my problem, please?" Shelly interrupted.

"Do you think Justice would lie?" Carla asked.

"I don't like it, but I guess she has to be lying. I don't know why she would, though. Maybe she just had a nightmare and thought she saw someone standing outside her door. Kids have nightmares and irrational fears. I just wish Macy wasn't such a bitch all the time;

now she's going to accuse me of this bullshit in court."

"Girl, I'm sorry. Custody battles are awful," Carla said. "Just talk to your daughter, that's all you can do."

"Or kill your wife," Chance said.

"Or that," Carla chimed in. "At least you have us to help you hide the body."

"Don't be volunteering me for crazy shit," Chance said.

"It was your idea."

"Exactly, an idea. One that I support, but will support without any involvement." He pointed a long green-painted fingernail at Carla.

"I think I'm going to go home after this drink," Shelly said. "Thank you both for trying to cheer me up, but I really just need to try and figure out my life and why I'm missing twenty-four hours of it."

"Good luck to you," Carla said. She and Chance held up their drinks.

"I should be heading to meet my date soon anyway," Carla said. "Mama's gonna eat good tonight."

"Girl, bring me some takeout," Chance called.

"I'm not eating for two," she snapped.

"Hmmm …" he looked her up and down. "Are you sure?"

"Take it back," she yelled. She lifted the butter knife beside her glass and clutched it in her hand.

"Jesus, you guys, people are watching," Shelly said, holding up her drink and guzzling all of the fruity vodka.

When Shelly parked her white Ford Focus in the

garage, she sat there for a while, staring at the empty shelves on the wall. When Macy moved out, her tools were some of the first things she packed. Macy was always so handy to have around the house; she could fix anything. The garage was so clean without her equipment. It was completely bare. She closed the garage door with the car still running. She laid her head on the steering wheel, and her emotional walls crumbled away as she erupted like a broken dam, water streaming from her eyes.

After a minute, she turned off the car. She entered her house through the garage and proceeded into the laundry room. She ignored the piles of clothes and moved on into the kitchen where she immediately grabbed a bottle of whiskey. She carried it with her to the den, and collapsed on the couch.

"Screw Macy," she said out loud.

She didn't even ask me about the situation, she thought. *She just made assumptions, as she always does. I hate her. I hate her. I hate her.*

She repeated it ten times in her head before taking a long swig straight from the bottle. She grabbed the pills sitting on the class coffee table and took two before taking another swig. Painkillers and alcohol were never advised, but she didn't care. Numb was what she wanted to feel. She stood up and grabbed a glass from the kitchen to put an ice cube in it before she poured a heavy draught of whiskey. She returned to the couch and sat down in front of the TV. She turned on the evening news, and after a few minutes, she fell asleep with her drink in hand.

Shelly jolted awake when she heard banging. Her glass fell from her hand, and whiskey spilled onto the carpet.

"Shit."

The banging resumed, after a brief pause. It took her a few moments to realize that it was coming from the front door. Someone was knocking on it loudly.

Why the hell don't you just use the doorbell?

She picked the glass up and set it on the coffee table before hurrying toward the front. The clock on cable box revealed that it was after nine.

Who would be pounding on my door this late? Macy? She has a key.

There was a third round of pounding on the door; this time it was even louder. This wasn't the polite knock of neighbors, or friends waiting outside with wine, this was aggressive. It made her pause when she reached the foyer.

"Who is it?"

She tried to listen, but she couldn't hear anything from outside. It was quiet. Several moments passed in silence. The silence stretched on too long, and she thought that whoever it was might have left. She turned to go back to the den. She only made it two steps before there was one hard bang against the door, causing her to jump and cry out in surprise. She hurried to the door and flung it open angrily.

"What the hell is …?"

Her voice trailed off when nothing greeted her but the night's cool breeze. There was no one outside. She flicked on the porch light and glanced around the yard.

"Hello!" she called.

She thought of the teenagers next door and cursed under her breath again. Someone was screwing with her. Then she noticed the white cardboard box at the base of the porch. She reluctantly took a step outside to get a closer look. The box was beat up and soggy. It hadn't rained, so she was unsure of where the moisture came from.

Everything within her told her not to touch the box, but she found herself kneeling and placing her hands on the lid. She lifted the thin flap, and both of her hands came up to cover her mouth. She gagged and her butt hit the concrete as she scooted away from it and scrambled back inside the house, slamming and locking the door. She leaned back against the door, sucking in air, but no matter how many breaths she took, her lungs felt empty.

It couldn't be. It wasn't possible. How did it get here?

She sunk to her knees, and tears fled her eyes and ran down her face. She couldn't shake the image from her mind. What was inside hardly resembled a stuffed tiger. It was no longer orange but a soggy brown, and pale maggots wriggled in and out of holes in its mouth, like they were feasting on a corpse. Its black beady eyes were missing, and wet stuffing oozed out like pus.

She hadn't seen the tiger since she was a young girl, but it was undoubtedly hers. The stitching on its upper right paw was unmistakable. Her father had torn its leg off during one of his drunken fits.

The last time she'd seen it was her father's funeral. She tossed it into his coffin before they forever sealed away the face she despised most in this world. She'd loved the tiger, having it since before she could remember, but she grew to hate the furry animal after she learned that it had been her father's first gift to her.

It was impossible. It couldn't be here. Who would dig up her father's grave? Who would want her to remember the horror that had been her upbringing?

She moved to the den where she found her cell, and she called the police.

When the police came, she gave them a statement and told them where the decayed stuffed animal had come from. They asked her three times if she was certain it was the same toy from her childhood, and she assured them that it was. Her father's grave was two states over, and it was hard to believe that someone would deliberately desecrate a grave and then drive eleven hours just to torment her. It was an awful lot of work for it to be a simple prank. This took effort and an investment of hatred.

"Ma'am, are you sure you've told us everything?" one of the officers asked skeptically. "We can't effectively investigate this unless you give us all the details. If this is really a toy that's been buried with your father, then it's someone wanting to stir up old wounds, someone you know. We'll have a local officer check your dad's gravesite to see if there has been any foul play."

There was only one person who came to mind who might have done it, but she couldn't pull herself to name him. She told the police she had no idea, which only seemed to make them doubt her further. She didn't want them to interrogate her older brother; he'd not only deny it, he'd use it as an opportunity to lash out at her further. No, if it came to it, she would deal with him herself. But why, why after all these years would he suddenly want to hurt her?

"I'm sorry. I wish I knew, really. I blocked a lot of this stuff out, ya know. My childhood wasn't exactly milk and cookies."

"Well, call us if you think of anything. Call your relatives. Help us help you. We will notify you once someone looks at your father's gravesite."

She nodded.

"Keep your doors and windows locked, miss."

When they left, she locked the door and went upstairs. She passed her daughter's room. The door was open, and she could see the radiance of the moon outside the window. Her daughter's screams echoed in her head. Justice had been terrified that morning. Could someone have actually been in the house? It was unlike her daughter to just make up stories, and that horrid display Shelly found waiting for her outside, gave her doubts that it was all just a nightmare. *There's only one way to find out.*

She closed her daughter's bedroom door, and went to her room. She sat on the edge of her bed and clutched her phone in her fist, trying to sum up the courage to call her brother, Greg.

How could the bastard do this, she wondered. Why would he do it? She hadn't spoken to him in over six months. He'd never expressed hatred toward her before, only indifference. They were never close, even as children. They didn't share the same admiration for their father. As kids, Greg worshiped their father, but she hated every atom that made up her father's revolting body.

When their father was killed, she told Greg not to mourn him. She told her brother what the man had done to her. To this day, Greg never believed her. He told her to shut up about it, threatened her for ruining their dad's good name. After that, things between them were never quite the same.

She leaned over to the nightstand beside her bed and opened the top drawer. She pulled out a half-empty bottle of vodka and took an absurdly long drink, before pressing the call button on her phone. It rang and rang and rang until it went to voicemail. She hung up and immediately called again.

"Answer me, you fucker," she growled.

She slammed the bottle on her nightstand and let her anger fester into false courage. It rang four times, and then she heard his groggy voice on the other end.

"Hello?"

"How dare you," she snapped. "You evil bastard."

"Oh my god, Shelly, are you drunk?" He didn't wait for a response. "Of course you're drunk, you're always drunk. Why are you calling me?"

"Don't act like you don't know!" she screamed into phone. "What kind of sick fuck … where are you?"

"Look, I don't know what's going on with you, and I don't care. I'm going back to bed."

"Where are you?"

"In Cleveland, where else?"

"You're a liar!"

"You're such a shit show, Shelly. You need help. Are you drunk like this in front of your baby girl? Get help, sis, you really need it. Otherwise, you really are going to lose custody of her. In fact, you probably should lose custody. It's no wonder Macy left you."

He hung up.

Shelly bit her lip so hard she could taste blood. She called him back again, but he must have turned off his phone, as it went straight to voicemail. His words hurt, but not as much as his sick prank.

"It had to have been him," she said aloud.

The vodka bottle taunted her from atop the nightstand. She stared at it for a while, and then buried her face in the pillows to muffle her scream. She bit down on her pillow, the fabric absorbing her saliva. She wanted to claw and chew and rip apart everything around her, to topple her dresser, smash the mirrors on her closet doors, throw her flat screen TV through her window, and set the room on fire while her body melted away into an ashy smear on her bed.

Who would give a shit, she wondered. No one would even notice. Her own daughter wouldn't even notice. Macy would rejoice. She imagined the afterlife and being reunited with her dead relatives. She shivered, and silently prayed that when she died, she would be greeted with nothing but darkness.

Shelly woke up screaming. Sharp pain slithered up and down her leg. She threw off the comforter and found fresh blood soaking into her white sheets and a piece of glass was protruding from her thigh.

Mirror glass. It was everywhere. Broken bits of mirror were scattered on the floor, morning sunlight glistening off them. Several pieces surrounded her on her bed. Her closet mirrors had indeed been shattered, no, exploded.

Her room had been trashed. Clothes were torn apart, scattered across the floor, and every drawer of her dresser had been removed, their contents spilled out. Her television was still mounted on the wall. It didn't appear broken. She hissed through clenched teeth as she pulled the piece of glass from her leg.

What the hell had happened? Had she done this?

She remembered the tsunami of grief and rage inside her head from the night before, but she didn't remember this. She hadn't done it. She'd gone to bed. She'd cried herself to sleep.

This wasn't her. But it had to have been. Her brother didn't have a key to her house. How could she have slept through someone tearing apart her room? It had to have been her. She'd wanted to destroy everything around her, and in a blacked-out drunken stupor, she'd done just that.

She carefully maneuvered herself out of bed and half-hobbled, half-tiptoed across the glass- covered floor, blood following her to the bathroom.

The bathroom remained untouched. She removed her clothes, grabbed toilet paper, and held it to her wound. She wondered if she needed stitches. She sat on the edge of the bathtub, and turned on the cold water. She rinsed the wound and the blood from her leg.

"What is wrong with me?" she asked aloud.

Tears began to form in her eyes, but she didn't let them escape. She blinked them away, refusing to pity herself. She was dumb enough to destroy her own belongings, so she would just have to deal with it. Once she'd rinsed and washed her leg, she hobbled into the tub to take a shower. She couldn't turn the water up very high without causing her leg to sting even more. For all that blood, the cut wasn't as big as she'd thought, and she was relieved she probably wouldn't need to go to the hospital.

Once she was clean and dry, she placed a big square bandage over her leg. She danced around the floor of her room, dodging shards, and found a green sundress that wasn't torn or covered in bits of glass. She hated dresses, only suffering through them when she had to, and this was one of those times.

She hurried downstairs to get some water, but froze when she reached the bottom of the staircase. She'd walked right past it. She glanced back up the stairs, but she couldn't see her daughter's bedroom door. But she knew it was open. She was sure she closed it last night. She wouldn't have drunkenly wandered in there too—would she?

She felt desiccated, like dehydrated fruit, and her head throbbed. She ignored the pain for now, and moved to the kitchen. She considered pouring a shot of vodka into her glass of water; she knew that would help her headache, and maybe soothe her anxiety, but she was furious at herself for what she'd done. She had to clean her disaster of a room before her daughter returned home tomorrow; otherwise she'd probably get another threatening call from Macy.

She chugged her first glass of water and then poured a second before moving to the couch. She grabbed half of a stale bagel from a bag and turned on the morning news. She was expecting political scandals, but instead got a murder investigation. Her phone vibrated on the coffee table. It was Carla.

"Good morning," Shelly said, surprised to find her voice harsh and raspy.

"Ugh, you sound awful, are you still sick?"

"No, just hungover."

"Well, grab a drink and turn on the news, honey," Carla said. "This will make your day. Poor bastard. He did have a lot of bad juju coming his way thought."

"I am watching the news ..." she said. That's when she read the text at the bottom of the screen.

"Holy shit." She took a long sip of water, wishing it was booze.

"Yeah, somebody did him in, real dirty business. That's why he wasn't at work Thursday or Friday. It took them a couple of days to find him, dead in his home. They say his head was mashed like a potato."

"This is unbelievable," Shelly said. "Elliot was a dick, but he didn't deserve that."

"I wonder who did it," Carla said. "Maybe one of the fifty people he's fired this year? Maybe his wife?"

"He didn't have a wife," Shelly said.

"How do you know that?" she asked.

"Because he asked me out last week right after screaming at me. I think he overheard Macy and I were separated."

She decided to leave out the part where he got a little handsy in the office.

"Makes sense since he was single. What woman in her right mind would love that asshole other than his mother? You should have gone out with him, though. Job security, you know how that works."

Her phone vibrated in her ear; she pulled it away so she could see the number. She couldn't recognize it.

"Hey, Carla, let me call you back." She clicked over to the other line and gave a cautious "Hello."

"Hello, is this Shelly McNeil?" a man asked.

"Yes, it is. May I ask who is calling?"

"It's Officer Lopez; I'm with the Cleveland PD. I was asked to investigate a gravesite this morning and, uh, there was nothing out of the ordinary. Your father's grave wasn't dug up. Grass is as green as can be."

The phone shook in her hand. That was impossible.

She switched the phone to her left hand and held it to her other ear.

"I'm not sure how that's possible. I know it was the same …"

"Look, I'm not entirely sure what happened to you, but I'm telling you what I saw. I just finished my report, and I figured I'd give you a call."

She nodded into the phone as if he could see it.

"Well, thank you anyway. I'll have to think about this some more."

"Well, good luck to ya. Stay safe."

She hung up the phone and sprawled out on the couch. She didn't know if she should feel relieved or terrified. It had been the same damn stuffed animal. Or someone had made a replica of it. Again, the only suspect that left was her brother. She hated the thought of speaking to him again.

She didn't call Carla back, but instead carried the broom and dustpan upstairs to start cleaning up the glass in her bedroom. She wasn't going to let him scare her, and she wasn't going to allow herself to fall deeper into self-destruction. She'd be productive today. She swept the floor of her room, careful to check every square inch of the floor, under her bed and dresser. The last thing she wanted was to have her baby girl step on a shard of glass while playing. She'd never forgive herself.

She threw her bloody sheets in the garbage and found fresh linens in the hallway closet. She was both saddened and furious to find that two-thirds of her clothes were ripped or shredded. So much money had been wasted in her drunken act of needless destruction. She was only hurting herself, like she'd always done.

By the end of her cleaning, she'd finished the rest of the vodka on her nightstand. She sat down on the couch, with her laptop and a glass of a cheap wine, to browse the web for new clothing. She'd wanted a new wardrobe, and now she had her chance. Somewhere in the back of her mind, she knew she shouldn't indulge herself. Her phone vibrated again as Carla called a second time.

"I'm sorry I didn't call you back. I was dealing with some personal stuff," she said.

"And do I have some personal stuff to tell you. I was distracted earlier by that dickbag being offed, but on the brighter side of life, my date last night was spectacular."

"Oh, do brag," Shelly said sarcastically.

"Look, I know you have sworn off men, but not all of us have embraced the puss just yet. And if you'd meet a man like the one I went out with last night, you might change your mind."

"I'm assuming he was handsome."

"Handsome, financially stable, and smart, too. You never get the trinity; it's always like pick two and settle."

"Oh, praise the Lord," Shelly laughed.

"And he had a big one."

"You slept with him the first night?"

"Of course not, honey, just a little foreplay. I know to always leave them wanting more. I just gave him a little taste."

"Good for you, Carla. I'm happy you met a decent guy for once."

"Yeah, it was great. He's the tall, dark, and handsome type too, deep voice. Too bad he's from Cleveland, I don't know if I can do the long-distance thing. But he says he plans to move out here soon."

"Did you say Cleveland?"

"Yeah. Oh yeah, you are from Cleveland."

"What's his name?"

"It's Greg. I don't know his last name but …"

Shelly ended the call right then and there and dialed her brother's number.

"You lying son of a bitch," she snapped when he answered. "And don't you dare tell me that I'm drunk; I know you are in town. How did your date with Carla go?"

"Calm down, calm down. I wanted to surprise you, but then you bit my head off last night and I chose to just stay away. You've got some demons, sis."

And you're one of them, she thought.

"But why now? And why Carla?"

"That was just a coincidence. I saw her in a picture with you a while back on your profile, I thought she was pretty, and then she just so happened to message me on this online dating app when I got to town. I wasn't creeping on her, okay? It just happened."

"How long have you been here?"

"I got in two days ago."

"Two days? You were planning to surprise me, yet you

never called and you've been here for two days?"

"Look, I'm here because Macy called me," he said seriously. "She called me and told me you've gone off the deep end. She's worried about you, and she's worried about your baby girl being around you. I went to visit her first, and then …"

"And then you decided to harass me?"

"Look, I don't know what happened to you last night, but whatever it was I had nothing to do with it. I was with Carla until late last night, remember? Now I'll wait and let you think about that and how stupid you sound accusing me."

"But if it wasn't you, then …"

"Then you have someone else trying to harass you. Look, do you want to meet up? We could grab dinner, or just a coffee. It's been a while. I'm sorry I haven't been around much. We can just talk."

"I …" She looked at the wine glass on the table. "Just give me a couple of hours, please. We can meet at this little Italian place nearby. I'll text you the address."

"How about I just pick you up?"

"Fine." She hung up without another word.

If it wasn't him, then who could have done it? It couldn't just be a coincidence. She stared at the wine. She didn't want to be drunk when her brother got there. He was clearly only there for an intervention, and he didn't want to give him further reason to doubt her.

Carla called back again, but Shelly didn't answer. She wasn't prepared to tell her that Greg was her brother. That would only lead to questions about him and her family, and she hated talking about her family, almost as much as she hated her family.

She drank a glass of water and decided to take a sobering nap. She set her alarm for two hours and texted her brother to pick her up in three hours. She sprawled out on the couch and pulled down the pink rabbit blanket that was draped over the back of her couch. It was sinfully soft, but not long enough to cover her whole body. She was asleep in less than a minute.

When she awoke, there was a pounding on the door. It startled her awake, and through her foggy mind, she found her thoughts returning to the night before. The pounding resumed after a few moments. Why didn't he just ring the doorbell? Sunlight still shown through the window.

She climbed off the couch and moved toward the door. Every step she took, sent razors up her thigh. She lifted the skirt of her dress and saw the bandage had absorbed quite a bit of blood. She'd have to change it again before leaving. The knocking became more erratic, but louder. She tried to move faster but stumbled and collided with the door. The knocking stopped. She gripped the handle, flicked the lever, and opened the door.

When Greg arrived at Shelly's house, he was surprised to find the door already open. He hadn't been there in a long time, and he hesitated before going inside.

"Shelly," he called.

He poked his head through the door and glanced around the foyer. He heard a ringing somewhere in the house.

"Shelly," he called again, louder this time.

He stepped into the house and closed the door behind him.

"Are you ready?"

There was no answer, but the ringing continued. He walked down the narrow hallway to the living room, and found the source of the noise, but no Shelly. Her phone sat on the coffee table, a wake-up alarm sounding loudly while the phone vibrated on the glass. He picked up the phone and dragged the digital red clock across the screen with his finger so it would stop ringing.

"Shelly?" he called louder.

She had to be upstairs. He called her name again when he reached the stairs, but there was still no response. He shook his head and cursed under his breath as he moved up the first few steps.

"Why the hell can't you just be ready for once?" he muttered lowly under his breath.

He passed the bathroom and paused in front of Shelly's daughter's room. The door was open, and he heard something inside. It sounded like scraping of an object on wood, and panicked whispering.

"Shelly?"

He peeked into the room and covered his hand with his mouth to muffle his cries. In the dim, eerie glow from sunlight seeping in through the dark green curtains, Greg saw his sister. She was naked and babbling incoherently. A torn dress lay at her feet, absorbing the blood that was dipping down her leg, blood that trailed all the way up between her thighs.

She dropped the wooden softball bat from her hands. The end of it was bloody. She let out a scream of uncontrollable rage when she saw him, a scream unlike any he'd heard before, like multiple screams at different pitches all escaping her mouth at once. She raked her nails across her bare breasts, clawing into her own flesh.

Greg wanted to flee, to run from the house, but reason overcame his fear and disgust. He rushed her, grabbed her, and tried to subdue her. She flailed, kicked, and screamed. She bit down hard on his shoulder, and he yelped in pain. He threw her down on the ground, forced her head away from him, rolled her onto her stomach, and pinned her. In an instant, the screams stopped, and she spoke in a voice that wasn't hers. It was masculine, deep and demented.

"She's mine," the voice said. "She's still my little flower."

Shelly stopped moving … stopped talking … stopped breathing. Greg realized he wasn't breathing either and sucked air into his lungs. His heart was pounding, and his shoulder burned from where she had bitten him.

"Shelly?" he called, out of breath.

He lowered his head to the side of hers to get a better look at her face. Her eyes were shut.

"Come on, sis, wake up." He shook her.

Her eyes flew open, and she moaned in pain.

"What the hell, Greg? Get off of me!"

It was her voice this time. He didn't move. His brain wasn't fully processing what had happened, and he felt as if his body had shut down. She screamed, not in rage this time, but terror.

"Oh God, please, no! Please, no. Get the fuck off of me!"

Her words jolted him out of his trance, and he jumped off her.

"Shelly, what the fuck just happened?"

She lifted herself to her knees, struggled to stand. She crab-walked back until she was cowered in the corner. She wrapped her arms around her knees and clutched them to her chest.

"What the fuck were you doing to me?"

"Me? I didn't do shit to you. You were crazed. You just … you just …" He dropped to his knees as he couldn't find his words. "Fuck, what just happened? You were hurting yourself."

"I …" Her voice trailed off as she saw the blood on the floor, felt the blood on her legs. She felt the flesh under her fingernails.

"You were scratching yourself, and you …" his eyes went to the softball bat. "We need to get you to the hospital."

She rocked back and forth, breathing heavy. She couldn't remember how she'd gotten into her daughter's room. She couldn't remember whatever horror had just occurred. She tried to think, tried to remember what had happened. She wasn't drunk, not anymore. Her nap had sobered her up, she was sure of it. She remembered waking up to go to answer the door, and then everything was a blur of sunlight and blood.

"Shelly," he said louder. "What just happened was … well, it wasn't like anything I've ever seen."

He got up and took a step closer.

"Stay the fuck away from me, you bastard," she snapped.

"Jesus, I'm trying to help you."

"You've never tried to help me," she said. "Never. So why now? Why come now? Why were you … how did we get in here? What did you do to me?"

"I didn't do anything to you," he yelled. "I just got here, your door was open. I came upstairs, and I found you in here, torturing yourself. You were babbling and screaming, but then you talked, but it was like a different person was talking. You said, "She's still my little flower.""

Her eyes widened with horrified recognition.

Shelly's blood turned to ice under her skin, and she couldn't move. Her anger had shriveled up as fear bubbled to the surface. The missing day of her memory, the decayed stuffed tiger, the destroyed bedroom, the words little flower, her brain filtered through the last horrifying twenty-four hours … old memories roared back to life. Buried horrors of her childhood came bursting through the grave of her mind with newfound fury.

"Shelly, you have to know I'd never …" Greg started, but she didn't let him finish.

"Something is happening to me," she said, interrupting him. "I can't explain it. I've been having blackouts, and someone left me a horrifying package."

"What kind of a package?"

"I thought it was you. It was my old stuffed tiger. I buried it with Dad. Someone dug it up and returned it to me, only I checked and Dad's grave wasn't dug up, but it was the same damn tiger with the same stitching. I can't remember Thursday at all, or even last night. I, I destroyed my bedroom."

"We really need to get you some help. Maybe you should see a psychiatrist or something for these blackouts."

"It's not just the blackouts," she said, frustrated. "Someone or something is doing something to me."

"The package and the blackouts aren't necessarily related."

"I said little flower, right? That's what Dad used to call me before he …" She couldn't say it. "It's not a coincidence. The stuffed tiger, little flower, it's like he's coming back to haunt me."

"That's crazy." His voice sounded unsure, as if part of him could have been open to believe her, yet he seemed to choose reason over superstition.

"I don't know why I'm talking to you about this anyway. Just leave."

"Now wait a minute."

"You have never been there for me!" she yelled. "Never. You called me crazy when I was a little girl, and you are calling me crazy now."

"I didn't call you crazy just now, I said."

"It doesn't matter what you say. Just get the hell out of my life."

"I'm sorry, okay?" he yelled. "I'm sorry." His voice softened during his second apology. His eyes revealed his grief. "I'm so sorry."

"Why now?"

"Because it's been eating away at me for so long. I wasn't there for you. But I wanted to be here for you now."

"You didn't believe me."

"I didn't want to believe you, but I knew. I knew. I couldn't, I just couldn't handle it back then."

"You couldn't handle it?" she screamed. "You? How the fuck do you think I felt? How do you think I could handle it, a little girl whose own father defiled her again and again and you couldn't handle it?" she spat. "You knew this whole time? You despicable bastard! You are a coward. I hate you! I hate you. I hate you!"

"I'm sorry." His voice was barely a whisper.

"Great, you're sorry. Take your apology and shove it!" She stood up and stormed out of the room. He averted his gaze, sunk back to the floor, and wept. She'd never been so angry in her life. She wanted to punch him, to stab him, even.

"You better be gone by the time I get out of the shower!" she yelled down the hallway. "Never speak to me again. I mean it, or I swear I'll fucking kill you." She slammed the door.

She cried the entire time she was in the bathtub. Warm

water stung her tender skin, and her body wouldn't stop shaking. Once she felt clean, she dressed in sweatpants and a light T-shirt. Pain encompassed her entire body. It hurt to walk; it hurt to sit still. She forced herself to leave her room, just to check her house to make sure she was alone. As she instructed him to do, Greg had fled. She locked the front door, and moved to the kitchen for some water. She was starving.

She searched her refrigerator, found some takeout from a questionable date, and sniffed it. Deciding against it, she searched the freezer. She microwaved two chicken burritos and carried them to her couch along with a glass of wine.

Don't think about it, she repeated over and over in her head, as if that would prevent her mind from focusing on the strange horrors that had suddenly encompassed her life.

Don't think about it, and maybe it will all go away.

Her hands were still shaking as she took a bite of the scalding burrito. She didn't want to be alone, yet she would rather sit there, terrified, than have to endure her lying scumbag of a brother for a moment longer.

How dare he think a simple "I'm sorry" would fix everything, not after all these years. Her sadness and fear were overcome with anger once again, and she decided it felt so much more comfortable being infuriated. All these years and he knew, he knew. He called me a liar because he didn't want to admit that his daddy was a fucking monster.

She grasped the wine glass in her hand and took a long drink. Her hands clenched together when she heard the now-familiar pounding on the front door. She accidently crushed the glass between her fingers, and red liquid and broken glass spilled all over her. She looked at her fingers, covered in red, but she didn't feel any pain. A few glass slivers lay on her skin, but the glass didn't pierce her.

Who the hell was it?

The pounding came again, four knocks this time. Fear creeped back into her mind, and she got up and ran upstairs, instead of to the front door. She slammed her bedroom door, locked it, and moved to her bathroom to rinse the wine and glass from her hands. She looked at her disheveled, miserable face in the mirror.

"GO THE FUCK AWAY!" she screamed when the pounding came again from downstairs.

The moment her words ceased, she jumped through the air, both hands coming up to her face, as the pounding somehow moved, mid-knock, from downstairs and outside the front door to upstairs and outside her bedroom door.

It was impossible.

She was silent, and frozen. Three long moments of stillness felt like forever, and then the angry, constant slamming of fists came down on the bedroom door. It was so loud and so hard that she thought the door would crumble away.

Her phone, where was her phone? She cursed when

she realized she had left it downstairs. She shut the bathroom door and locked it, turned off the light, and backed away into the corner, between the toilet and bathtub. The light from the bedroom peaked through the crack under the door. She knew hiding was useless. Whatever the hell it was, though she was sure she knew exactly what, or who, it was knew exactly where she was.

"It's not possible," she murmured to herself.

The pounding subsided, and she heard the door of her bedroom creak open somehow, despite being locked.

"I missed you, my little flower," a voice called from outside the bedroom door.

A voice that was dark, low, and unmistakable. Tears, streamed down her cheeks. She let out a loud sob, and shook in the corner.

"Please, God, no. Please. Go away." Her voice was less than a whisper.

A shadow blocked some of the light as it stood outside the bathroom door.

"Come out, my flower, or I'll come in and pluck you."

Darkness consumed the light outside as the doorknob began to rattle. Its words came slowly, as if he were savoring them on his dead lips.

"I love you. Don't you love your daddy?"

There was a click as the door unlocked itself. She screamed as it slowly opened. The smell hit her first. It was more than just death, but also mildew, and sulfur all mixed together. She couldn't breath as the stench seemed to carry a weight with it, and flooded her lungs like water. In the darkness, all she could see were his eyes, soggy, milky, and luminescent.

As she coughed and gagged, it pounced, grabbed her legs with wet, rubberlike bony fingers, and dragged her toward the bedroom.

Carla carried her coffee mug with her toward her front door.

"I'm coming, I'm coming, Jesus Christ, I'm coming!"

Her pink slippers slid across the hardwood floor. She only wore a thick pink robe, but she figured whoever the hell was repeatedly ringing her doorbell this early deserved to get whatever view she had available. When she opened the door, she dropped the coffee cup, hot liquid splattering both of them.

"Shelly, what the hell happened to you?"

Shelly collapsed in Carla's arms, weeping and shrieking. She was hysterical. Her clothes were torn, her body was bloody, and she was covered in cuts and bruises. Carla struggled to pull the poor woman into her house.

"I can't understand what you are saying; please just try to calm down."

She set Shelly on the floor and closed the front door and locked it.

"Who did this to you? I'm calling the cops right now."

"No!" Shelly cried. "You don't understand."

"You're hurt, you're bleeding, and you need a doctor."

"They can't help me," she cried, shaking her head frantically. "It's not a someone … It's a something."

Carla's face turned from worried and sympathetic to confused.

"You aren't making any sense. Were you drugged again?"

"No," she yelled, frustrated.

She inhaled deeply, trying to slow her breathing. She knew she sounded nuts. She breathed in through her mouth and out through her nose.

"Just give me a minute."

"Okay, well, let's give you that minute in the bathtub."

She reached out her hand to Shelly. She neglected to tell her that she reeked. Carla had never smelt something quite like it, and standing near her friend was starting to burn her nose.

"Let's get you cleaned up, and then you can try to convince me not to call the police or a doctor."

Carla placed a towel and a change of clothes by the sink in her bathroom and left Shelly alone to get herself together. She went down the hall and made another pot of coffee, making sure to have plenty for the both of them. She resisted the urge to call Chance, wondering if he could be another voice of reason for Shelly or if his involvement would only agitate her further. She drank her first cup of coffee and poured another, wishing she had beignets to go with it. *Shelly won't be mad if Chance comes over if he's got beignets.* She decided to call him.

"Girl, get your ass up and over to my apartment right now!"

"What's going on?" he muttered, his voice groggy and low.

"Bring beignets."

"I know your lazy ass isn't calling me for some damn beignets right now."

"No, no …" Her voice got lower. "Shelly showed up at my place covered in blood and in hysterics. She's in the shower right now. I don't know what happened, but I've got the coffee covered. I figured the poor girl could use some sweetness in her life right now, that's all. It's only a block away from you."

"Well, shit, honey. I'll bring the tequila, too."

"You know we're gonna need it."

Shelly spent almost an hour in the bathroom before she limped her way into the kitchen.

"You called Chance?"

She brought her hand up to her forehead in frustration. She didn't want everyone to think she was a nut.

"Relax, honey, I brought beignets. You know you want one … or two … or three."

"Here is your coffee," Carla said as she floated across the tile floor and put an arm around Shelly's shoulders, forcing the mug into her hand.

"We are here to cheer you up," Chance said, blinking rapidly with his luscious lashes.

"And get all the dirt," Carla joked. "Just tell us who to kill; whoever did this to you is going down."

"You guys are the worst," Shelly said quietly, but her

lips curled up into a small smile.

She felt a tiny bit relieved with the two of them around. Carla guided her to the little round table, and she sipped the hot coffee. Shelly added some cream and a little sugar, and took a beignet from the bag.

"You want some chocolate?" Chance slid over a little dish of melted chocolate.

Shelly felt like a child for a moment, the way they were treating her, but she was hungry and allowed herself to indulge on the doughnuts while the other two stared at her expectantly. Carla was still in her bathrobe, but Chance had somehow found the time to glamour himself up with green glitter eyeshadow, tight leather pants, and a green top, complete with an emerald necklace and matching earrings.

"Are you ready to tell us what the hell happened to you?" Carla asked when there were no more sweets left.

Shelly released a heavy sigh.

"I don't know if I can say it." She turned her head to face away from them, and stared out the window at the brick wall of the building beside them. "It's just too crazy; you'd never believe me."

"I've heard it all," Carla said. "Just spill it already. I can't take all of this suspense."

Then her tone softened, revealing her genuine concern.

"I can't help you unless I know what is going on."

Shelly hesitated. "I don't think anyone can help me. It's like I'm damned."

"Honey, you're going through a lot, but your life isn't

over," Chance said. "You can bounce back."

"No, Chance, I mean literally. I'm damned. I can't even find the words to explain what horror is haunting me."

She turned from the window to face him, and her frightened, panicked, defeated expression struck him. His sympathetic smile vanished, and his eyes went wide with not just surprise, but almost with recognition.

"What's going on, girl?"

"You know how people say your past will come back to haunt you? Well mine has, in the very literal sense."

"You mean someone from your past came and attacked you?" Carla asked.

She nodded, her eyes still on Chance. Liquid formed in the corners of her eyes.

"My father."

"I thought your father was dead?" Carla said.

Shelly shivered and covered her face in her hands.

"He is dead," Chance said, answering for Shelly.

"Oh Jesus, I forgot you were into that woo-woo crap," Carla said, rolling her eyes. "Shelly, as your friend, I'm just going to come out and say it. I think you need some professional help."

"Please," Shelly begged. "You have to believe me. I don't think I can survive another attack. I've been having more blackouts, and he's been … doing things to me that I don't even remember. I thought it was just me, I thought I was just getting drunk and doing these things myself, but my brother, he saw it happen, he couldn't explain it either. But then last night he … he came to me, my dead dad, he came and the things he did to me …"

Her head went down on the table, hard, and she let loose, wailing sobs.

"Hey, hey," Carla was up instantly and rubbing the poor woman's back. She looked at Chance and mouthed the words *she's lost it*. "It was just a dream."

"A dream can't do this?" she screamed jumping up from the table, startling her friends.

She motioned to the cuts and bruises on her body, before she collapsed back into her chair, and onto the table.

"It was just like when I was a kid," Shelly said into the table.

"What did your father do to you as a kid?" Chance asked.

"Do I really have to say it?" she answered.

Her head came up, and she tried to wipe her tears and snot away with her hands. Carla handed her a paper towel.

"How did your father die?" Chance asked.

"Some freak accident," Shelly said. "It's still really fuzzy. I can't remember what happened, but I do know that I was there. He died in my bedroom."

"Holy shit," Carla said. "I'm so sorry, I had no idea."

"He was a monster! The things he did to me, and no one believed me. No one would help me. I was only ten years old. I prayed, I prayed and prayed that he would go away forever, that he would die, even. And then he did."

"Well something listened," Chance said.

He looked at her as if he suspected that she wasn't telling him everything she knew. He waited for her to say more, but she didn't.

"But it wasn't anything benevolent. Not from the signs of what's currently going on with you."

"Demons, ghosts, spirits, whatever, they don't exist," Carla said. "This is crazy talk, and you are just encouraging her."

"They do exist," Chance said to Carla. "I'm not saying I haven't 100% written you off as a crazy person, though." His eyes locked on Shelly. "But there is only one way to find out."

"What, a séance?" Carla groaned. "Not in my house."

"What's the matter, you suddenly believe now?" He rolled his eyes. "No, I'm not summoning any dark shit to appear," Chance said, shaking his head and his hands in an "absolutely not" gesture.

"I'm not crazy. But I may be able to help you help yourself, but you have to trust me as well as yourself."

"Shelly, I can't even begin to imagine what you've gone through, but you are just having a breakdown, and that's understandable. It's trauma, that's all. Let's get you some help, or counseling, or some good meds, and you'll be back to normal in no time."

"I will," Shelly said, looking up at Carla. "If this doesn't work, then I'll get help."

She turned to Chance.

"I'm desperate, and if you can help me in any way, I'm willing to try it. And if nothing happens, you can drive me to the loony bin. I don't know what else to say."

"Whatever it is, if it does exist, it has attached itself to you. I can't get rid of it. But you can if you face it."

"I can't," she squeaked.

"Your father is dead," he said. "It's not your father. It's only appearing as your father because that is the source of all the darkness in you. These things feed off it."

"Where are you getting this shit from?" Carla demanded.

"My grandmother," he said proudly. "And a few books, but not the kind you can find on Amazon."

"Are you guys really going to go through with this?"

Shelly and Chance both answered with silent stares.

"Jesus. All right, whatever, but if she doesn't start floating and spewing green shit from her mouth, I'm calling bullshit on the both of you, and then I'm driving you both to a mental institution."

Carla sat down, defeated.

"And I need a shot or five right now." She yanked Chance's tequila bottle off the table and carried it to the refrigerator. "Do I have any limes?"

"Why now?" Shelly asked. "Why, after all these years, is this happening now?"

"It probably never left you," Chance said. "It was just waiting. Waiting for you to find a new source of pain and anger. It takes a lot of energy for beings like this to appear and affect our plane of existence. Some things in your life have been building up over the years, and something set you off, and now you are releasing it back into the world."

"You actually believe me? Why? I probably wouldn't."

"As Carla said, I'm into that woo-woo shit. It kind of runs in my family."

The way he said it was as if he wanted it to be true, as if this would prove and thus satisfy something within him. Carla poured a shot of tequila for each of them.

"I already expressed that I'm not doing this shit sober."

"We will have to do it at my place," he said. "And we will have to wait until tonight, of course, when the moon is in full bloom."

The word "bloom" made Shelly cringe. She wondered why they had to wait until nightfall, but she didn't bother asking questions.

"Well then I guess, let the day drinking begin," Carla said grumpily and brought the shot of tequila up to her mouth.

"I should call Macy," Shelly said quietly as she got up. She eyed the shot of tequila in front of her but didn't take it. "I can't let Justice see me like this."

She placed her hands on her sides, expecting to find her phone in one of her pockets, but then realized she wasn't even wearing her own clothes, and her phone was probably somewhere in her own house.

"Can I use your phone, Carla?" she asked.

"Yeah, it's in my bedroom on the nightstand. The passcode is my birthday; real original, I know."

Shelly escaped the kitchen and moved to the bedroom down the hall. She found the phone and called Macy. It rang until it went to voicemail. She hung up and immediately called again, knowing that Macy never answered for numbers she didn't recognize.

"Who is this?" Macy answered, a little too aggressively. "Remove me from your call list."

"It's me," Shelly said. "I'm sorry, I don't have my phone with me."

"Oh well, that's not a surprise," Macy scolded.

"Look, I don't want to fight. I don't have the energy. I just really need you to keep Justice for a few more days."

"What?"

"Please. I'm sick, and I don't want to get her sick. Just a couple of days."

"Of course I'll keep her," she said as if it were the obvious response. "Besides, she likes staying with me more anyway. She told me that last night. Call me when you have time for your daughter." She hung up.

Shelly clenched the phone in her hand, and resisted the urge to throw it against the wall. It wasn't her phone. She couldn't break it. She inhaled deeply through her mouth, and then exhaled through her nose before dropping the phone onto the bed. Instead of screaming, or crying, she just sat down on the floor, her back against the wall.

Did her daughter really prefer Macy over her? The words stung more than she could stand. It broke her in a way she'd never experienced, yet she couldn't cry. She was all cried out. She couldn't find sadness within her, so instead she focused on the pain, and pain turned into anger, and that anger warmed her bruised body.

"She wants to take everything from me," she whispered aloud to no one.

"Justice is all I have, and you can't take her from me."

She banged the back of her head against the wall with a thud, and the sound and impact made her jump. She closed her eyes, clenched her teeth, and listened to the rhythmic thump thump thump as she began to rock back and forth, her head knocking against the wall harder and harder each time.

"Before we do this, there are two things you need to know," Chance began.

They spent most of the day relaxing, drinking, and finally napping. Shelly slept like a rock for five hours before they finally packed up and relocated to Chance's apartment.

"The first, is that this entity is feeding off of you; which means it needs you, which means that you can cut it off. You are stronger than it. These beings can't function without us, at least not on a physical level."

Shelly nodded glumly. She didn't feel strong at all. The previous night she had been helpless to defend herself against the demonic assailant.

"The second is that none of this is your fault. Your father's death wasn't your fault. What he did to you was horrifying, and you were, and still are, the victim in all of this. The evil men do lives after them."

"The good is oft interred with their bones," Carla chimed in.

"I didn't know you were so cultured," Chance said,

his tone changing from serious to amused and proud.

"I can get down with some Shakespeare."

"Yeah, I bet you like to be shaken and speared," he said.

"Mmm hmm, Mommy likes."

"Guys," Shelly said, cracking another half-smile. "Focus. I'm about to probably venture into the darkness and never return, and you guys are joking about getting speared."

"Well, when all this shit is over, we'll get you a nice big spear," Carla said. "One from that new store down the street." She paused and her cheery tone faded. "We're just trying to brighten the mood, honey."

"I know, and I thank you," she said. "I love you both so much."

"All right, love," Chance said. He placed both hands on the sides of her head. "I need you to trust me. I'm going to put you in a sort of trance."

She nodded and closed her eyes, as if expecting him to tell her to do so. The pressure of his hands on her face vanished, and after several moments, of silence she opened her eyes.

Chance was lighting candles in the room. There were several different colors, some red, some black, some gold. Then he held some type of sack over one of the flames and started burning whatever herbs were inside of it.

"When do we start chanting?" Carla asked.

"Bitch, sit down. If you aren't going to take this seriously, we don't need you to participate."

"Okay, okay, I'm sorry," she said defensively. "I'll try to keep an open mind."

He dragged a wooden chair across carpet and sat down across from Shelly.

"Maybe we should bind your hands," he mumbled more to himself than to anyone.

"What for?" Shelly asked.

"Never mind, forget it. If it gets too intense, I'll pull you out of it."

Her palms and armpits were sweating now. She had no idea what he was about to do to her, yet she was too afraid to not let him do whatever it was. Nothing could be worse than what she'd seen last night.

"Relax," he said, staring at her. She must have looked terrified. "You have to calm down and stay focused, and stay strong. Be brave, and you will be able to stare this thing down, and kick it the hell out of your head and your life."

"You make it sound so simple."

"It's not. But I'll be talking you through it the entire time. Just listen for my voice, and I'll be able to pull you back out. The further you get away from my voice, the harder it will be to come back. Don't let it lure you in—instead, bring it to you."

"This isn't making any sense," she said.

"It will. Now close your eyes."

She obeyed and did her best to relax her muscles.

"Breath in slowly through your nose, and then out of your mouth."

She focused solely on her breathing, trying to clear

her mind of all thoughts. It mostly worked, except for the lingering sting of the betrayal she felt from her daughter. The smell of whatever he was burning intensified. She assumed Chance was wafting it into her nostrils.

"I want you to think back to when you were just a little girl," Chance said.

I don't want to, she almost said aloud.

"I know it's hard, but I want you to visualize your old house."

She sighed and tried to remember her childhood home. She remembered it was blue, an average-sized home with a two-car garage, and a little backyard. Her room was upstairs, beside her father's room. Her brother's room was in the basement. There was a third bedroom upstairs, but he'd wanted to claim the bottom floor to himself and all his childish adventures. It was so much space for a little boy, and he'd hardly ever let her go down into his lair. It also meant that there was an entire floor in between him and her, so he might not have heard her cries for help.

"Describe your bedroom," Chance said. His voice already sounded further away.

She tried to visualize her bedroom, and it was easier than she'd thought. She saw it, as if she were standing there in the doorway. Her bed was in the far corner of the room beside the window. A narrow desk sat a few feet from the foot of the bed, topped with a dozen tiny collectable stuffed toys. Her dad would bring her a new one frequently, his attempt at apologetically soothing her.

The first two had been received with naïve endearment, but then they quickly became soft, squishy symbols of so many tormented days, like tick marks on a prison wall. She hated them. At night, the animals would stare at her with their tiny, beady, black eyes and laugh.

Her tiger had been her comfort. She'd had it since before she could remember. She'd clutch it, cuddle it, sneak it in her backpack, and take it everywhere with her. It wasn't until her father's untimely death that she'd learned that he'd been the one to give it to her. It was her birth gift. It was as big as her when she was born. The tiger sat atop the pillows of her bed, staring at her.

Somehow, within her memories, she took a step into her bedroom. It was all so real. Too real. The more she visualized the room, the more it solidified, and the more she felt like she was actually standing in the room.

The sunlight in her bedroom window faded to black, and she reached out and touched the wall. She could feel it. She was there, in her room. She flicked the switch on the wall. The room filled with light, and she moved deeper into her room. She eyed the choir of stuffed animals on her narrow desk. She shivered. She wanted to burn them, or to tear their heads off and empty their insides out on to the floor. In the center of them all rested a photo of her smiling mother.

Her mother had had the most perfect teeth. She'd died of cancer when Shelly was only six. She turned away from them and stared at her closet. The sliding doors were mirrors, and she recalled every single time she'd seen her own wide, horrified, pain-filled eyes reflecting back at her in the dark. She stared at herself in the mirror, only she wasn't her grown-up self. She was short and skinny, her hair poking out from an old baseball cap. She wore a white and blue jersey, and had glittery lip gloss, and she was missing two teeth. She was a child again in her old bedroom.

On her bed sat her old stuffed tiger. She shivered. She'd loved the animal once and had clung to it after her mother died, thinking that it had been a gift from her. Shelly remembered that she even used to talk to it. Once it even talked back, or had she dreamed it? That's when she remembered that the damned thing had a name.

She approached the squishy beast as if it were a real predator. It had spoken to her. She remembered it clearly now. The sun was setting, and she was outside in the back yard, playing alone on the swings that her father built for her and her brother. Her cheeks were wet from tears. The tiger sat on the swing beside her. She was pleading to the cosmos that someone would come and take her away, that someone would rescue her from the clutches of her father. Little Shelly swung higher and higher before she heard the chains of the swing beside her groan. Her head turned to the left, and she saw the swing moving on its own.

She dragged her feet across the ground on her way down and tried to slow her swing, and then on her return, she jumped and landed on her feet, stumbling and almost falling. She spun around to face the phantom swing, and stared into those dark beady eyes. The swing kept moving back and forth at a steady, deliberate pace.

"Mom?" she asked softly.

There was no response, just the sound of the chains and the wind. She wasn't afraid, yet she thought she should have been. *Mom's dead*, she thought. Ghosts aren't real, she was old enough to know that. But then what was moving the swing?

"Are you here to play with me?" she asked.

There was still no response, but the swing kept moving. Feeling unnerved, she backed away from the swing, and turned toward the house. She'd get her brother and show him. Maybe he would know what to do.

As she took her first steps toward the house, she heard a soft plop behind her. She turned and found the toy on the grass, flat on its back, staring up at the sky. The swing flailed awkwardly at the sudden loss of weight. She hesitated, but she found herself tentatively approaching the stuffed animal, half expecting it to move. It didn't. She knelt beside it and poked it in the chest.

"Are you still there?" she called, as if she were on the phone that went quiet due to a lost signal.

"Yes," it said, dragging out the sound of the word. Its voice was wispy.

"Are you my mommy?"

It took several seconds for it to answer, but it said "no".

"Then who are you?"

"You can call me Asmodeus," the stuffed tiger replied.

"She's asleep," Carla said. "She's not even responding. Did you drug her?" Carla snapped her fingers in front of Shelly's face a few times.

"No, I didn't drug her," he said defensively. "Well, not exactly." He thought about it for a few seconds. "Okay, maybe a little if we are really getting technical … by definition. But it's part of the process. She definitely went under a lot faster than I had intended. Deeper, too. But that's what it takes to resolve this. It forces you to face yourself."

"Let me guess, you haven't done this before."

"It's not every day someone gets haunted by dark spirits."

"Jesus, the poor girl should have never trusted you. This takes exposure therapy to a whole new level."

"Relax, she's fine. Except talking her through it is going to be—"

His voice was cut off by a sudden loud banging on the front door. They both jumped in surprise. The pounding stopped after a few seconds.

"Who the hell is that? A pissed-off ex? You haven't been blowing straight guys again, have you?"

He reluctantly moved toward the door.

"Who the hell is it?" he called.

In response, the door began to rattle under rapid and ferocious banging against the wood. Chance stumbled backward in shock.

"I'm calling the police," Carla said, fumbling for her phone in her pocket.

"Just wait," Chance said, putting his hand up.

She almost didn't hear him over the constant thud against the door. He clenched his fists, and took a deep breath. He moved to the door, unlocked it, and flung it open, as if he was ready for a fight. The knocking stopped instantly. Carla slowly moved behind him to see who it was, but there was no one in the doorway. Chance poked his head outside and looked up and down the empty hallway.

"Fuck this shit," Carla said. "I don't know what the hell you just did, but this is just too much. Wake her up now!" she demanded. "We're leaving."

He closed the door and locked it, although he knew the lock wouldn't do much good. Whatever had been banging on their door was already inside with them.

"Shelly, come back …"

She heard a voice call out to her, a voice she recognized, but couldn't quite place. The voice sounded so far away, not just outside her room, but outside the house. She picked up the stuffed tiger on the bed and hurled it against the wall.

She tried to reply to the voice. Just as she opened her mouth, she heard a noise, like a heavy weight on an old wooden floor. The creaking sound stretched across the room, and the ceiling lightbulb above her head fizzled and died at the same time as the bedroom door closed, consuming her in darkness. Not before she caught a glimpse of what had been hiding behind the bedroom door.

"No, get out!" she cried. She backed up, breathing rapidly, hyperventilating.

"Awe, don't worry, baby," the man who had been hiding behind the door called. "It's all going to be okay. Isn't it always okay?"

She backed up against the bed, and almost fell back on it. She caught herself, as if preventing herself from falling off a cliff.

"Please just go away, Daddy," she begged, her voice barely a whisper.

"But you didn't lock the door," he said. "You always lock the door now, like you're in here doing something you don't want me to see. You aren't doing anything you don't want me to see, do you? You aren't being naughty, are you?" His voice was smooth and snakelike.

Her eyes were adjusting to the darkness, and his familiar face slowly came into focus, his dark eyes, balding head, and his short, unkempt beard.

"No, I haven't been bad, I promise. Please just leave and go to bed."

"Why aren't you in bed? It's so late." He took two slow steps toward her.

Her mouth quivered as she struggled to speak. Her cheeks were wet from tears.

"I, I don't want to go to bed."

"It's time for you to go to bed, my little flower. Let's put you to bed."

"No!" she screamed and tried to run past him, but his arm outstretched and caught her, and swung her around into him.

"Stop fighting me. I just want to put you to bed. You need your sleep."

She screamed, and his free hand came up and covered her mouth. She kicked and flailed to no avail, and struggled to breathe through her snot-filled nose. He flung her up and dropped her onto the bed, his weight crushing down on top of her.

"Stop fighting. Just go to bed!"

She bit his hand, and he cried out before slapping her so hard that she thought her head might fly off. Her screaming stopped, and her tears froze in her eyes. The painful sting somehow numbed her into silence. She didn't move.

"That wasn't nice, Shelly." He stared down at her, not in anger, but in disappointment.

He pulled the cap off of her head.

"Why do you always look like such a fucking tomboy?" he demanded. "I already have a son. I never should have let your mother put you in all those sports."

Put me in sports? she thought. *I wanted to play sports. It had been my decision.*

"You need to start acting like more of a lady," he said. He paused, his tone softening. "You love your daddy, don't you? Daddy just wants you to go to sleep.

You need your sleep."

He lay down beside her.

"I'll stay with you until you are asleep."

His hands brushed her hair. His hand came down over her face, and his fingers trailed her cheeks and lips.

Please, she thought silently to herself. *Please, kill him, kill him, kill him, kill him.*

She repeated it in her mind over and over again. Then she called his name out loud, just as he told her to.

"Kill him, Asmodeus."

"What?" her father whispered in her ear.

She didn't answer. She just stared up at the creature that suddenly appeared on the ceiling, its skin covered in tar, its eyes like burning embers, its white fangs glimmering in the dull light from the window.

"Goodbye, Daddy."

"What did you say?"

He sat up and stared down at her. He didn't notice the creature standing upright on the ceiling, unaffected by gravity, and reaching out. Its body dissolved into black and red smoke, as if the smoke itself was carrying fire within it. The smoke slithered down and into her mouth. It tasted of ash, but it warmed her from the inside. Her vision became blurry, like she was looking through a distorted screen, little red dots of light floating around in front of her vision like fireflies.

"I said goodbye, Daddy. I'm his now." She spoke, but it wasn't just her voice.

There was another voice speaking with her, a horrible throaty voice, and when she had said the word "his", that second voice had instead said the word "mine". Her father's face revealed confusion before fear. Her eyes went black, but her pupils glowed like hot coals.

He didn't have time to react, didn't have time to scream. She reached her tiny hands out to the sides of his face, and twisted. His neck broke with a satisfying crack, and then his body fell off of her, off of the bed, and onto the floor with a thud.

✎

"Wake her up," Carla snapped. She had her arms crossed defensively over her chest.

"I'm trying, but I can't." Chance was hunched over, gently slapping her face. He'd been calling her for over a minute.

"Well, maybe if you didn't drug her," she cried out, both anger and fear in her tone.

"It's not like this. It doesn't take someone this deep. It's like she's in a coma."

He lifted one of her eyelids and jumped back. The whites of her eyes were black. The dim light of the room intensified, and suddenly the entire room felt hot.

"This is something else," he said. She was so still she looked dead.

"Chance," Carla called, her voice barely above a whisper.

He turned around to find her looking around at the candles. One by one, the flames were intensifying, shooting straight up into the air, the wax melting rapidly until the wicks burned out, the wax spilling over into pools.

"This is really happening …" She sounded dumbfounded. "We need to leave," she said. "This is fucking insane."

Sweat began to form on his head and face.

"I can't, not yet," he said, his voice determined despite his fear. "Shelly isn't going to be able to go anywhere until she beats this thing. I can't just leave her. You should go."

"This whole place is going to burn down," she said, stepping away from another intensifying flame.

"It won't. It's just trying to scare us," he said, his voice soft and reassuring. "It needs her, so it won't kill her in a fire."

Shelly suddenly started to twitch in her sleep.

"Shelly," Chance called louder, returning to her side. "Shelly, can you hear me? You can do this; you have to fight it."

"No, get out!" Shelly cried, only her voice wasn't her own; it was much too childlike. "Please just go away, Daddy."

"Oh fuck," Chance said, grabbing both of her shoulders and shaking her.

"What's happening?" Carla asked.

Shelly's head snapped to the side as if something had

hit her, her hair flailing around her head. Then she was still, her eyes still closed. But then she started to speak again, so quietly that it was difficult to hear her.

"Kill him! Kill him! Kill him! Kill him!" she repeated, her voice monotone, unaware and trancelike.

"Why won't she wake up?" Carla asked.

"Kill him, Asmodeus," Shelly said.

And then Carla screamed. The room went dark, as the candles flashed out. Chance didn't see what Carla saw, at least not entirely, but he caught a glimpse of a dark figure in that last millisecond of candlelight, and he knew it was there. The room smelled of smoke and tar.

Shelly's eyes opened in the dark, although the only reason Chance knew her eyes were open was because her tiny pupils were glowing like the last embers of a once-blazing fire.

"She's mine now."

Words spoken in a masculine, horrible voice escaped her mouth, and without hesitation, Shelly hissed and swung her fist, striking Chance in the jaw. He staggered back and fell on his butt in surprise. Shelly was up on her feet a second later. Carla cowered down beside the couch, her legs crumpling beneath her.

"Where's my little flower?" the dark voice snarled. "Come out, come out, Mommy wants to see you."

"Shelly, fight it, don't let it win," Chance called.

She stared at him with those flaming eyes, arms hanging, her fingers outstretched like claws. She sniffed the air, and then turned and sprinted to the front door of the apartment. She ripped it open, and disappeared into the hallway, the lights outside immediately flickering. Chance jumped up and dove for the door. He looked outside, but Shelly had already disappeared around the corner.

"I think I know where she's going," Carla said, out of breath.

Macy awoke to Justice tugging on her hand. Startled, she ripped her hand away from her daughter, and yanked it up to her own face, as if to defend herself from an attacker.

"Mommy," Justice called, her voice filled with panic.
"Justice, you scared the hell out of me." She took a deep breath and tried to calm her throbbing heart.

"What's wrong?"
"The man is back; he's in my room," she whispered.
"Honey, what are you talking about?" She remembered that Justice had complained about a man staring at her from the doorway at Shelly's house.
"The man, he followed me. He's in my room."
Macy immediately felt bad for accusing Shelly of

bringing strange men home. *Fuck, I've been such a bitch to her,* she thought. The divorce hadn't been easy on any of them, but she admitted to herself that she should have talked to Shelly about it instead of accusing her so suddenly. She promised she'd try to do better, or to at least not scream at her so often.

"You just had a bad dream, honey. There is no one in your—"

Her voice was interrupted by a sudden bang from somewhere in the house. Justice screamed, but abruptly covered her mouth. She shrunk down to the floor beside the bed. Macy jumped up and moved to the closet beside the bed. She opened it and fumbled around in the dark until she found the hammer she had used earlier to hang photos around the house She moved to the doorway and glanced back at the bed. Justice had disappeared underneath the bed.

"Whoever the hell you are, get the fuck out of my house!" she screamed into the hallway. "I've called the police."

It was a lie, and she immediately regretted not actually calling the police. Her cell phone was on the nightstand, beside her bed. She was about to move back into the room, but saw movement in the hallway. A silhouette of person stood in the center of the hallway. Two beady red orbs that must have been eyes stared back at her in the dark. She gasped, and instantly the creature moved from the center of the hallway, and pinned itself against the wall until it seemed to become a part of the wall itself, dissolving into a shadow.

The whole encounter lasted a mere two seconds, so quickly that she blinked several times, thinking that it must have been some trick of the moonlight. She dove forward to the light switch, just a few feet from her, but before her hand could reach it, something grabbed her hair from behind, and yanked her backward, her body slamming against the wall, her head cracking the plaster.

Inside the room, Justice was hiding under the bed. The sounds she heard were unbearable. Her mother was screaming in sheer agony and terror. There was banging and crunching, the sounds of bones breaking, and sloppy, wet splattering. Justice couldn't cover her mouth to muffle her cries and both of her ears, so she chose to cover her ears. She bit down on her lips, inhaling through her nose. The sounds lasted for minutes.

Justice watched the doorway, waiting for whatever horror that was outside to come in. She waited, and waited. Eventually she took her hands from her ears and listened to the stillness. She didn't see any movement. Justice knew that her mother wasn't coming back. The silence stretched on for an eternity, and she still didn't move. There wasn't a sound or movement in the hallway.

Maybe he's gone, she thought. *Maybe it just killed Mommy and then left.*

She decided that she wouldn't dare move until sunrise.

She'd hide all night. She was thinking this as a hand reached down from on top of the bed, gripped her by the hair, and dragged her, kicking and screaming, from under the bed.

Shelly hovered over the corpse of her father. How could I have forgotten its name? How could I have forgotten that I was the one who broke my father's neck?

She didn't feel a drop of remorse; triumph was more like it. He was a sick bastard, and she'd put him out of his misery. She only wished his death had lasted longer, as long as the torment he had put her through. A shadow moved beside her, and she turned to the bed. The tiger stared at her, unmoving, sitting atop the covers.

"It was you," she said aloud.

She glanced down at the body at her feet, and it seemed to shrink slightly, but then she realized that it was because she herself was growing. She wasn't a child anymore.

"Asmodeus," she whispered.

Her father's corpse twitched, and his dead hand reached out and grasped her ankle. She screamed and tried to kick her foot free, but the grip only tightened. Her father raised his head, and his eyes were came alive, burning red in the night.

"Are you still my little flower?"

"Get off me," she cried. "You aren't my father!"

"Noooooo," he moaned long and loud. "I am not your father. I am your redemption."

She gripped the bed for support and pulled her leg, struggling against his grip.

"You are mine," he hissed.

He reached out his other hand and grasped her other leg, tugging, and pulling her down onto the floor. He slowly crawled on top of her, flicking his tongue in and out of his mouth rapidly.

"Please, let me go," she cried, defeated.

"Let you go?" he cackled, a deep, distorted laugh that sounded like it was coming from everywhere.

"You are nothing without me. I saved you. I always save you. You're nothing without me."

His hands slid up her legs, and his weight pressed down on her.

"You don't remember, do you? Let me show you."

Moving faster than her eyes could see, he was no longer at her legs, but gripping the sides of her head. He lowered his face down to hers, and shoved his lips against hers, his tongue slithering into her mouth so deeply that it reached her throat, and then everything went black.

She gagged as if she was choking, free falling into a void. Eventually a tiny light appeared, a light that expanded and intensified as she fell toward it. In an instant, she was a kid again on a playground, standing beside a pole that kids could slide down on from the tower of the park. Her old elementary school came into focus in the background, beside a field where some kids were playing soccer.

She had wanted to play, but four of the girls had prevented her from being able to join a team. She could only remember one of their names, Keri. Keri and the other girls hated her, and she was never sure why. Keri would trip Shelly or embarrass her every chance she got. Shelly remembered that she'd waited in line to play Four Square, and when it was finally her turn, Keri intentionally planted the ball right in Shelly's face. The girls all laughed and then shouted,

"You're out."

Shelly didn't have many friends, so she sat alone in the tower, too timid to even wander across the plastic bridge to the yellow slide. Most kids enjoyed recess, but she had slowly grown to hate it. She liked the sports she got to play after school because they weren't involved with any schools; they were private leagues. There weren't girls like Keri there to convince everyone that she was a freak, or call her a boy.

She looked down at the field, somehow watching two scenes at once with the same group of kids. On one side, she watched alone from the tower as the children played soccer. Keri stole the ball from a smaller boy and took the ball downfield with ease. On the other side of the tower, Keri and her followers were surrounding Shelly by the tetherball pole. Shelly wanted to play, and had asked if anyone wanted to be her opponent. Like a pack of lionesses descending on their prey, they challenged Shelly, but not to a game.

"Shelly, you should just kill yourself because you're such a pathetic freak," she said. "Here, I'll help you."

Keri pushed Shelly against the pole and wrapped the tether ball around her neck. She struggled, but the other girls grabbed her arms to prevent her from fighting back.

"See, now all you have to do is hang here," Keri said. "Then you can go on to hell where all the other dikes go."

Shelly didn't even know what a dike was. They called her hideous and told her that she looked like a man, and then they finally retreated to class as the bell rang, leaving the poor girl crying and alone. She unwrapped the rope from her neck and sunk to her feet.

Her teacher had been too busy watching the kids on the field to notice what happened until after the girls had already left, but Shelly was too broken to even tell her what had happened.

Now Shelly remembered, all too well, that Keri died the next day; a tragic child suicide.

"No," she whimpered.

"Oh yes," an invisible voice whispered in her ear.

When Shelly heard the news, even as a kid, she felt only relief. Now, looking back on the scene, she felt only guilt.

"You couldn't."

"Little cunts like her don't deserve to live," the demonic voice said angrily. "My poor little flower, being withered away by those bitches. I'd feast on all their souls, even to this day, if you'd only ask."

"But I didn't ask," she said, tears forming in her eyes. She still stared down at the now-empty playground, as the sun rapidly set. "She was just a dumb kid."

"But you wanted it. You wanted her to die, and I heard your heart because it's mine."

The sky darkened, and next she found herself standing outside of a house that she didn't recognize.

"Now where am I?" she asked.

"Where we were a few days ago," the voice said. "Just open the door."

She didn't have to reach out to touch the doorknob, because the door slowly creaked open on its own. Without walking, she was moving forward and into the house. Blood. So much blood. It was everywhere. The walls, the floor, the couch, the chair, the television. She saw herself, rolling around in it on the hardwood floor, moaning in some deranged, trancelike euphoria.

"No, I didn't do this," Shelly said.

"We did this."

"Why don't I remember?"

"You weren't ready. Such a gory sight for a little flower. It's better this way."

She sunk to her knees and covered her eyes. She couldn't watch.

"Why did you kill Elliot?"

"We killed him," he corrected. "You wanted him dead because he was vile."

"No, no, no, this isn't me!" she screamed. "I'm not a killer; you are just using me!"

"I'm protecting you!" the voice yelled in her ear so loudly her ears vibrated and burned. "As I've done since you were a child. No one, no one, no one has been there for you the way I have."

"I don't want you to be there anymore," she cried. "Just leave. Leave me alone forever. Please."

She was begging. The response was a roar so loud that her hair blew around her head, and she covered her ears to muffle the sound, only to find that the roaring was inside her own head. The roaring shifted, growing higher in pitch as it softened until she recognized the sound of a car honking. Even with her eyes closed, she saw a brightness approaching, and she opened her eyes in time to see a car squeal as it swerved to barely miss her. Metal crunched against metal as the car ripped through the guardrail and off the side of the road, tumbling over a short drop and wrapping around a tree.

How did I get outside?

She stood up, barefoot in the road. It was cold, and

her clothes were tattered and ripped.

Where am I? she thought, shivering and disoriented.

She reached into her pockets to find her phone, but her pockets were empty. She didn't recognize the road, or see any other cars approaching in either direction, so she hurried over to the ruined guardrail.

"Please be okay," she prayed softly. But she knew—by the sound of the impact—that there wouldn't be any survivors. What she wasn't expecting was to see her brother's bleeding face sticking through the windshield.

A scream of grief, terror, and rage escaped her mouth. Laughter filled her head.

"He was almost as bad as your daddy. He knew, and he didn't even bother to help you. This was a faster end than he deserved."

"This can't be. Greg can't be dead."

"But he is," her brother's face said through the broken windshield, but it wasn't her brother's voice. "He's dead and rotting and burning."

"I don't want to see anymore!" Shelly screamed.

She turned from the car and ran downhill through the trees.

"But there's so much more," the dark voice said in her head.

As she neared the bottom of the hill, she found herself

standing in front of Macy's house.

"Oh God, please, no!" she cried.

She sprinted to the front door of the house and ripped it open.

"Don't you touch my fucking daughter!" she screamed.

Justice screamed and kicked as she was plucked from under the bed. She rolled over onto her back as something dropped down from atop the bed and onto her chest, pinning her to the ground. The hands released her hair, but grasped her skinny neck and squeezed. She stared up into the face of her mother. Justice's screams were cut off along with her oxygen.

Mom, please stop, she thought. *Why did her mother's eyes look so wrong, like they were on fire?*

Her lips were curled up in an angry grimace. Justice dug her nails into the skin of Shelly's skin, but the grip around her throat didn't loosen.

She whined, and cried, "Please, Mommy," but her voice barely escaped her mouth.

Why would her mom want to hurt her? Why would her mom want to hurt her other mommy?

Her head started to hurt, and there was nothing she could do.

"Mommy," she called … *or had she merely thought it?*

She was fading, and her eyes closed, as if she were going to fall asleep, but she was suddenly able to suck in air.

"Justice," she heard her mother's voice.

Justice coughed as she gasped for air. She opened her eyes to see her mother's face. Shelly's eyes were clenched tightly, as if trying to hold the flames within them at bay.

"Run, baby. Run away."

Justice struggled to scoot out from under the weight of her mother.

"You can't fight me," her mother hissed in a different voice, a man's voice. "I'm going to pull her pretty little head right off like a weed."

Justice fought, using all her strength to squeeze free while her mother babbled on with herself. She got to her knees and ran toward the door.

"Justice, wait," her mother said.

She hesitated in the doorway and turned to look at her mother, who was no longer on the ground, but standing, arms outstretched toward her.

"Everything is okay now. Come to Mommy."

The little girl glanced out into the hallway in horror, at what was left of Macy, and then looked back at Shelly.

She shook her head no.

"Come here, you little bitch!"

Justice screamed and sprinted into the dark hallway, slipping and stumbling forward on the bloody floor. Her hands shot out and caught her balance, and she scrambled back to her feet. She sprinted into the kitchen and ran to the back door. She grabbed the doorknob and twisted. It didn't open. She flicked the lock and tugged at the door, but it still wouldn't open.

"There's no escaping your fate, my little flower," a voice whispered behind her.

She spun around but found herself alone in the kitchen. The only sound was her quick, shallow breathing. Justice scooted across the wall to the cabinets and opened the drawer with the knives, the drawer that Macy always scolded her for touching. Justice grabbed a knife so big, she had to grip it with both hands. The blade shook in her hands, but she gripped it tightly. She took a cautious step toward the hallway, thinking she would try the front door instead. She took a couple more steps before she heard something topple over atop the counter behind her. Justice spun around and saw Shelly crouched down on the countertops, ready to pounce.

How had she moved so fast?

"What are you going to do with that, honey?" her mother asked.

"Leave her alone!" Shelly screamed, only the words didn't come out of her mouth.

Instead, she was screaming in her own head. She was staring at her daughter from the countertop, unable to control her body. Somehow, the tar-covered demon emerged from a dark smog behind her daughter. Justice didn't notice the demon behind her. It placed a tender hand on the little girl shoulders and caressed her cheeks with his claws. Justice wasn't moving at all, she was so still, it was almost like she was frozen in time, the child's horrified eyes locked on her mother, her little hands gripping the knife.

"Asmodeus, you have done enough!" She struggled to move, her body was twitching, and her lips quivered, but no sound came out. "You've hurt so many people, all because of me. Don't take my daughter from me!"

"She's not your daughter," the demon hissed, clearly hearing her thoughts. He as able to exist inside her, yet outside of her at the same time.

"She knows it too. She hates you just like everyone else."

"She is my daughter."

"She's Macy's daughter, or she was." He laughed. "She deserved what she got."

"I carried her in my body; she is my daughter."

I can't let this happen, not to my little girl. She had to fight harder. *How could she stop him?*

"She's a weed; they are all weeds."

The demon's body changed in an instant, and she was staring into the face of her father.

"You are a flower."

The image of her father sensually stroking the little girl's cheeks sparked her fury, and that fury ignited the fuel for her clarity of mind. Chance's words returned to her. This entity is feeding off of you; which means it needs you, which means that you can cut it off.

"I'm not your fucking flower, Asmodeus," Shelly ground out through gritted teeth, and this time her mouth did move, and she found her voice. "You can only exist because of me. I don't need you."

"You wouldn't have survived without me. You'd have cut your own wrists if I hadn't been there to protect you from Daddy, from Keri, from so many others. I saved your tragic little life."

"And now I'm ending it."

"You can't beat me, Shelly. You are mine."

"It works both ways," she said. "I'm yours, and you are mine. We are one, and I'm going to end it."

The demon's fiery eyes widened with the realization of her words. It growled, low and threatening.

"I will save my daughter."

"She's mine!" he roared, and she pounced, her body moving on its own, her fingers curled like claws ready to tear her own daughter apart.

But just for a moment, one single moment, she regained control of her limbs. Instead of attacking, her arms outstretched, as if attempting to give Justice one final embrace. She flung herself onto the knife in her daughter's hands.

When Chance and Carla arrived at Macy's house across town, there were several police cars already there. Carla had called the police as soon as they got into Chance's car, warning them that Shelly wasn't quite herself and might show up there, deranged and violent.

"Carla!" Justice cried out, sobbing, and ran from the police officer and into her arms.

"Oh my God, honey, I'm so glad you are okay." She hugged the little girl as she sobbed.

"Were you the ones who called?" a male officer asked, stepping forward.

"Yes, we are," Chance said.

"It was too late," he said grimly.

"What do you mean too late?" Carla asked. "We came straight here."

"She beat us here," the officer said. "It's a real mess in there. I've never seen anything like it."

"But she was on foot," Chance said in disbelief. "She couldn't have made it across town before us on foot. She didn't even have her car."

The officer shrugged. "You said you called the police

as soon as she left?"

Carla and Chance both nodded.

"What happened?" Carla asked. "Where is Shelly?"

"She's dead," the officer said. "I'm so sorry, but she's dead. The other woman in the house is dead too. From what it looks like, Shelly, you said her name was? She killed the other woman, and then this little girl here had to defend herself with a knife. We won't know all the details until the crime scene is fully investigated. I'll need to get a formal statement from all of you. How well did you know these women?"

"Shelly and I are coworkers," she said, "Oh Jesus, how is this even possible?"

Chance grabbed Carla's hand and gave it a tight squeeze.

"Mommy was two people," Justice said softly.

Carla's eyes widened, and she looked at Chance, mortified and grief-stricken, but also with the horrifying realization that true evil did, in fact, exist. He couldn't find words. He looked down at Justice with tear-filled eyes. He had failed to help Shelly.

I only made things worse. I made her come face to face with her demons, and it killed her.

Another car pulled in front of the house, blue lights flashing.

"I'll be back in a moment," the police officer said. "You'll all need to come down to the station."

Chance nodded glumly. Justice had lost everything in an instant. Chance wanted so badly to go back, to have another chance to save Shelly and her family. It wasn't fair. Shelly wasn't a bad person. She was innocent, and she was defiled by devils her whole life.

Poor girl, he thought as he watched Carla feebly attempt to comfort the child. *She's going to be traumatized for the rest of her life. But she is alive,* he thought positively.

"Mommy didn't want to hurt me, but she did at the same time. Mommy was there, but there was someone else in Mommy, too."

"Shhhh," Carla soothed softly. "Your mothers loved you. Both of them."

"I know," she said. "Said she loved me before she died. She said she was sorry. She said she wouldn't let him hurt me."

Chance breathed a half sigh of relief. Shelly hadn't just disappeared into darkness. She had remained, resisted even. He couldn't save Shelly, but Justice had been saved.

Justice would live on, and she would not fall prey to the dark. He'd make sure of it.

ACKNOWLEDGMENTS

This wouldn't be possible without a whole village of people who have helped, taught, encouraged, and pushed me. There are so many people to thank, and I'll start with Judith Briles, The Book Shepherd, for kicking me in the ass to start my publishing journey, my editor Barb Wilson who helped me improve my writing, my best friend Kelsey Owens who designed the book and helped me with branding, Philippa Burgess who gave me the bright idea of starting *The Horror Crew*, thank you Gary Audi for funding the first print run of this book, Elliot Tracy, for workshopping some of these stories with me, Jen Zelinger, for being my final copy editor, my mother, for asking me "How is the book coming along?" literally every few weeks for the last two years, Thanks Gem Boehm-Reifenkugel for taking my author headshots, my Dad for showing me the horror genre as a kid to lure me into reading, everyone in my family that suffered through reading all my childhood horror stories and encouraged me in my writing for as long as I remember, my friends for reading my stories and encouraging me, and lastly I'd like to thank my demons, for writing would not be possible without them.

ABOUT THE AUTHOR

Bobby Crew has been writing horror since elementary school. Due to his twisted imagination, his parents thought they were raising a serial killer, but thankfully he chose to keep the killing on paper only. He keeps his fingers in publishing as Executive Assistant to a publisher and author resource organization.

Bobby has big dreams of branching out into screenplay writing and intends to slice his way into the Indie horror movie sphere, as well as creating a publishing company that will feature horror authors.

He is easily accessible and you can chat with him at: **Bobby@TheHorrorCrew.com**, subscribe to **TheHorrorCrew.com** or follow The Horror Crew Facebook Page.

Stay tuned for his upcoming anthology podcast launching in 2020.

- GBRPhoto.com

Thanks Gem Boehm-Reifenkugel for taking one of
the only pictures of me that I have ever liked.

www.ingramcontent.com/pod-product-compliance
Lightning Source LLC
Chambersburg PA
CBHW021242060726
47590CB00005B/1866